BEY

BOOK ONE

WITHOUT HESITATION

TALIA JAGER

Without Hesitation
Beyond Earth: Book One
Copyright © 2017 by Talia Jager. All rights reserved.
First Print Edition: 2017

ISBN-13: 978-1547176427
ISBN-10: 1547176423

Editing by The Dirty Editor
Cover and Formatting: Streetlight Graphics

DEDICATION

To the people who believe that love is love and hope someday we will all be accepted for who we are.

ACKNOWLEDGEMENTS:

I give my love and thanks to my tribe. Without your support, this book wouldn't be possible. I can't thank you enough for the love and acceptance you show me everyday.

Thanks to the fans who have loved my other stories and inspired me to write this one.

Thank you to my team: Streetlight Graphics and The Dirty Editor for making this book awesome.

CHAPTER ONE

AKACIA

THE BAMBOO STICK CONNECTED WITH a resounding crack as Bristow raised his own to block my blow at the last second. I pressed my body weight on the point where the two bamboo sticks met, trying to overpower him. Our faces were inches apart, so close that I could see the sweat droplets as they formed on his brow. I felt him falter, a slight give in his resistance and then Bristow grinned and threw me off easily. I leaped back into a defensive posture.

"You're getting good," he said, mopping sweat off of his brow.

"Am I or are you just slow today?" I asked with a sneer.

We'd both been learning Kendo for a little over six months now. As my second it was necessary for Bristow to be ready to protect and defend me, and Kendo, the Japanese martial art that involved the mastery of a bamboo sword, was one of many. I had no reason to learn any sort of fighting, sword or otherwise, but it felt good to remember that my body could be used for something besides eating and sitting in on formal meetings.

Bristow was stronger than me, but what I lacked in strength

I made up with speed and agility. But today I could tell his head just wasn't in it, which was made even clearer when my shinai met the middle of his back with a thud, muffled by his thick body armor.

"Alright," I said taking off my helmet and dropping my weapon. "What's up with you?"

"What makes you think something is up?" Bristow pulled of his own helmet revealing his messy, russet-brown hair. He looked at me with his kind brown eyes—the same ones that often got him out of trouble with our caretakers.

I hit him with what he liked to call my sassy stare. "Come on, Bristow. I know you. Something is wrong."

"Can we go somewhere else and talk?" He gestured to the hovercraft by the tree.

Glancing at our sunstar, Roma, I decided that we had enough time until I was due for survival class. "Of course."

Seconds later, we were flying over waist-height grass in the fields, past the fruit-bearing trees in the orchards, and steering far from the dense forest until we reached a large body of water.

Bristow held out his hand and helped me down—not that I needed it, he was just being a gentleman. We sat on the boulders by the water, both of us chucking small stones at it and watching the ripples.

Finally, Bristow blurted, "I got an offer to go with Treg on their mission to Zoyter to trade. It's a small step toward my dream."

My hand froze in the air for a few seconds before I threw the stone. "You're leaving?"

"I haven't given them a definite answer yet, but yes, I'd like to go." He turned to look at me. "We're taught to live life to its fullest. Getting off this planet is what I want to do."

I wanted to be happy for him, but all I felt was sadness. "Is it so bad here?"

"No, Kace." Bristow was the only one who called me this. I supposed growing up together gave him the right. I was Empress Sparks to most people, Akacia to others, and close friends called me Kaci. "It's not bad. I just want to see the galaxy. Don't you remember our dreams? Remember how we used to talk about exploring off planet?"

"Of course I do. The mystery of what's out there, the beauty of other worlds, the excitement of meeting other species—if there are any. What's not to love?" I remembered the many times we talked about exploring the universe, going on trips, finding new planets. Being confined to such a small area for so much of our lives, it made us want to see the universe.

Bristow's parents had worked with mine. Besides being the Emperor, my father was also a scientist. They were all murdered in a failed attack to get control of our planet twelve years ago. I didn't recall the details very well, and nobody talked about it. But I did remember Bristow had been with me the day our parents were killed. Even at seven years old, he was kind and compassionate. When he should have been mourning his own parents, he had put his arm around me while I cried. When those in charge came for me, I demanded he come, too. They tried to separate us, but I had such a grip on his hand that they let him stay. He became my family.

From then on we were inseparable. Bristow and I spent the next nine years sequestered in the compound where we played together, went to school together, and trained together. Three years ago, when I had passed my sixteenth winter, Galton told me it was time that I took on all the responsibilities of being the Empress of Valinor.

"But?" Bristow coaxed.

"It's not safe. I worry about you. You're my best friend. I don't know what I'd do without you," I admitted. "Besides you are my number two."

"I'll be fine. Your guards are top of the line. They wouldn't dream of letting anything happen to the empress's best friend. And you have Galton for now. The plan was for me to step up when he retired."

Staring up into the violet sky, I said, "I could order you to stay."

"Kace…" His face fell.

"But I won't. Tomorrow isn't promised. We must live for today, without hesitation. So go, Bristow, but promise me you'll come back." I leaned my head on his shoulder.

"Of course I will. This is my home. You are my family." He kissed my forehead.

"Empress," a deep voice said after clearing his throat loudly. We both jumped up.

"Crikey, Galton! You almost gave me a heart attack."

"Apologies, Empress. You are needed back at the compound." Galton shot Bristow a look that made Bristow step back.

"Is everything alright?"

"There is a spacecraft hovering just outside our perimeter."

"Sorry, Kace," Bristow whispered on our way to the compound.

"Don't be. I had fun. No hesitations, right?"

"Right."

The compound was where I lived. It was mostly hidden in the side of a mountain just north of the village, Baile. The only part visible was the entrance, windows, and solar panels, and even those were camouflaged very well. I yanked my blonde hair out of the ponytail it was in and let it fall around my face. As I brushed the grass off my blue shirt, I noticed the dirt caked under my fingernails from gardening earlier. I attempted to pick it out as we made our way inside.

The walls of the compound were lined with pictures. There was one of Earth about a thousand years ago, before it was almost completely destroyed.

Next to it was a picture of the spacecraft my family owned and our planet's namesake, The Valinor. And alongside that picture was one of the commanders, my great-great-grandmother Malou. Malou became the first empress, a monarchial position that was passed down to the eldest child in the family. Bristow always said I looked like her. I had the same heart-shaped face and we shared the same dimple on our right cheek, but as far as I could tell, that was where the similarities ended.

The control room was where the action took place. Computers monitored our world as well as the galaxy around us. I stood in the middle of the room surveying all of the monitors. "What is it?"

"See here," Galton said, pointing. "This spacecraft dropped out of FTL and seems to be hovering just outside the warning point."

"Have you identified the spacecraft?" I asked, taking a step closer to the screen, hands behind my back.

"No."

"Have you hailed them?"

"Yes. No answer."

"Is it going through?" I twisted the ring I wore on my right hand; the one that had been worn by Malou and bore the family crest. Not a dainty thing at all, but one of the things I held close to my heart.

"We can't be sure."

"Do you think they're pirates?"

"It's possible."

"Could they be here because of the summit tomorrow?" I was supposed to be leaving in a couple hours for a summit with other Alliance members on the planet, Caipra.

"Doubtful."

"Recommendations?"

Galton stroked his chin. It was a habitual thing he did when he was deep in thought, but it was funny because he used to have a goatee and recently shaved it. So when he stroked his chin now, it just looked odd. "We can wait and see, or fire when the ship is close enough."

"Can their weapons reach us from there?" I inquired.

"Depends on what they have," Niam, our weapons expert, answered. "If they have a long-range missile, we could take a hit. Should we fire on them first? This behavior is already somewhat hostile."

Thoughts filled my mind as I stared at the screen. If we did nothing, they could attack, kill us all, and take my planet. If we fired on them, we could start a war. Neither option was good.

Valinor was a small Earth-like planet with three continents, the one we lived on, and two uninhabited on the opposite side. It had almost no axial tilt, giving it a mild, almost boring climate. Rich with amazing natural resources, it was located in a very central area of the universe. For those reasons, people always wanted to live here. We welcomed peace-loving people, but there were those who wanted to take the planet from us. The last time they tried, they killed my parents, leaving me Empress. Valinor was my responsibility. I had to protect it and the people living on it. Malou named our village, Baile, an Irish word meaning home.

"Vika? Any thoughts?" As my advisor and teacher, I trusted her on these issues.

Her sandy-brown hair was pulled back tight giving her a fierce look. "I don't think we should fire on them. They could be explorers or maybe they need help," she said, offering a more positive view of things. "They haven't crossed the line."

Galton didn't look happy, but he knew the decision was mine to make. "Empress?"

Looking at Galton, I answered, "Wait for now. Keep trying to make contact. Put the guard on alert. If they cross over the warning point without communication, take the ship out."

"Yes, Empress."

"What's the probability they just want to say hi?" I asked, with a hopeful shrug.

"Low," Galton answered, his mouth set in a grim line. "You should hide in case they are hostile."

I shook my head. "I'm done hiding. I understand why I had to growing up, but I'm no longer a child. I'm the Empress, and I will not go down without a fight. You've all trained me well. Have some faith now."

"My apologies, Empress."

Galton's mouth twitched at the corners and some semblance of a smile came to his lips. Asserting my independence and claiming my rightful place as Empress didn't come naturally to me and Galton often challenged me in this regard. I can only assume that he was somewhat proud of me for refusing to be hidden away like a child or some fragile girl.

Shifting my attention back to the spacecraft, I wondered who was on board and what they wanted. Was this the invasion

I had trained for all of this time? If they attacked, today could be the last day of my life. Oddly, that didn't scare me. Death was our fate. The only thing I worried about was my planet. If Valinor fell into the wrong hands, I had no children who would succeed me, no other family who could step up to take my place. And now Bristow wanted to pursue his own dreams and have adventures off planet...

"Galton, if they attack and I die today, what will happen to Valinor?"

"Your death is not an option, Empress."

I knew he meant well, but I needed to know. "Humor me."

His expression grew serious. "As you know, lineage is what controls that. You succeeded your father. Bristow succeeded his. But because you were both so young, I stayed on along with Vika until you were old enough. So, to answer your question, Bristow would become emperor if you died. That's of course assuming someone is left on the planet after an attack."

"And if he wasn't around for some reason?"

"We have no protocol for that particular situation."

"Well, maybe we need to create one and put it in place." I stole a glance at Bristow. His face was stoic. I knew he would fulfill his duties, but I also knew he'd hate it. Staring back at the spacecraft, one thing was abundantly clear: I could not die.

I had no idea what to do. Fire or wait? By earthyear 2507, most of Earth had been destroyed. The governments there came together to move human life off the planet in order to save the human race and spread life throughout the universe. It took another three hundred years to achieve that goal. People stayed behind on Earth to reverse the damage humans had done. They had made great strides, but still have a long way to go to bring it back to its former glory.

A few years after humans left Earth, they began to find planets that were habitable. Some people colonized those planets while others worked on space stations.

After humans began populating planets, it was soon realized some sort of law was required and The Authority was formed. Most of the universe had joined an alliance, though there were some that refused, and others that were rogue. There were criminals we called space pirates. They'd attacked spacecrafts, invaded planets, stole, and forced people into slavery.

My parents had believed in peace and joined the Alliance in hopes to maintain it. Our own people were loyal to us. I wanted to keep that going. Firing first could lead to a war. Of course, if they fired, that could lead to a war as well. We had to talk to them. It was the only option that resulted in peace.

"Hail them again." I walked to the window and looked up to where the spacecraft hovered. The sunstar had just set, making it difficult to see. Something else caught my attention. A soft blue glow appeared just over the trees. Nobody else noticed. They were too busy trying to figure out what to do about the spacecraft. I had the distinct feeling that it was just a distraction.

I took off, heading toward that light.

"Akacia!" Bristow yelled. I knew he'd come after me.

Limbs lashed at my legs and arms as I ran through the trees, toward the light. Hugging the shadows, I wove through the forest until I came to the clearing. A female around my age in a black protective suit stood there checking some kind of device in her hand.

She was beautiful. Her hair was just as long as mine, but was dark, smooth, and straight and framed her oval face perfectly. Her bright, golden eyes scanned her surroundings.

She turned slowly revealing an animal print tattoo that trailed from the back of her neck, down her right shoulder, and her arm all the way to her pinky finger. I took half a step toward her before common sense drew me up short. I had been hiding for a reason. I had no idea whether she was friend or foe. It was dangerous to go charging out there, even if the girl seemed to be alone.

The stranger was facing me again. Her eyes landed near where I was hidden.

Could she see me?

She smirked and, said, "I know someone is out there. Save me the hunt and I'll spare your life."

Somehow I doubted she spoke the truth.

I hunkered down, daring her to find me. I was ready for her. Slowly, carefully, she picked her way through the underbrush and made her way toward me. She knew I was here, but she didn't know exactly where. Remembering how important it was that I not die, I couldn't take any chances. As soon as she was close enough, I struck.

Just before my arm made contact, she shifted her weight and spun, stepping out of the way. She threw a punch, which I dodged easily, but then she continued to come at me and I blocked her over and over, until I made a misstep. While I was stumbling, she caught my cheek with her elbow then landed another blow to my belly. I countered, slamming my hand onto the bridge of her nose sending her backward. She stumbled but caught herself.

I launched myself at her, drove my body into hers, knocking her to the ground. We both fell in a tangle of limbs. She rolled, putting distance between us, and we both jumped back to our feet.

When she sprung forward again. I twisted, my back protesting the movement, just enough to get out of the way.

We exchanged quite a few blows before she finally clocked me one good time in the face then followed that up with a kick in the ribs that stole my breath. I collapsed to the ground grabbing my side. Not wasting a second, I swept her with my foot, hooking my leg around hers, and yanking back with all my might. Her bright eyes widened as she went down, landing on her back. I jumped on top of her and pinned her to the ground. Now that I was up close I saw that there were two more tattoos on the left side of her neck: an arrow with two Xs in the middle, and another simple symbol next to it.

"Who are you?" I demanded.

No answer, though her eyes were wide with excitement—like she was enjoying this.

My heart thudded roughly against my chest. "How did you get here?"

Again, she didn't answer.

Using her legs, she bucked up, throwing me onto my hands and knees. She kicked me down and sat on my back.

"What do you want?" I asked, face to the ground.

"Looking for you, Empress Sparks. I have to say I'm surprised to have found you so easily."

I froze.

"Even if your marking didn't give you away, I would still have known who you were." She pulled my hair up and examined the back of my neck where the two inverted V-shaped symbols, one under the other. Malou had worn the same mark and so had every eldest child since.

"I'm not afraid of you."

"You should be."

I grabbed the knife from my scabbard and stabbed it in her leg, careful not to let it go too deep. She let out a muffled groan and rolled to the side. I sprang back on her and put my knife to her throat noticing the long, jagged scar that stretched from her left ear almost to her chin.

"Why are you doing this?" I pressed the blade against her throat, nearly breaking the skin.

She hissed. "I do not have a choice."

Looking into her eyes, I saw so much more than hate. "If you jump back to your ship, I'll let you live."

Her eyes widened and the smirk on her face turned to a hard line. "You're stronger than I realized, but that decision makes you weak."

Fury tore through me and I pressed down on the blade. "You want me to kill you?"

"You *should* kill me."

Just then, Bristow charged into the clearing with his gun raised. I stood up and stuck my knife back in its scabbard. "Get up. You're coming with us. And you…" he said, directed at me. "What the hell are you doing running off like that?"

My eyes never left hers. Using the device she was holding in her hand when I first saw her in the clearing, she tapped the screen and disappeared.

I sank to the ground and gasped for air, terror taking the place of adrenaline that had dumped into my system. I'd been in fights before. Why was my body reacting this way? Was it her? No one had ever made me question myself or challenged me the way she just did. Who was she? And why did I want to see her again?

CHAPTER TWO

EVERLEIGH

N O MATTER HOW MANY TIMES I did it, jumping would always feel strange to me. The feeling of all your cells breaking apart and reforming in another place was unsettling to me even though I've been jumping over long distances since before I was a teenager. This time, like every time, I feared that I would reappear with my arms and legs in the wrong place. So like always, I waited until my feet were firmly planted on a solid surface before I opened my eyes.

I appeared on the bridge of my spaceship—a large room with windows, computers, and our workstations. My crew looked over expecting to see the empress with me.

"Where the hell is she?" Huxley Keenum, my second-in-command, asked.

"Couldn't find her," I lied.

"You weren't down there very long," Huxley accused.

"Someone saw me."

"Wait... You got caught? You? Everleigh Marsden, great commander of the Nirvana, got caught?" Huxley teased. Mischief sparkled in his green eyes.

"Shut up!" I shot him a look, my fist pounding down on

the counter. "We'll go back, but right now we need to get out of here. Give me some time to think."

They all looked at me like I had lost my mind and honestly I considered the possibility. What the hell had happened down there? Why didn't I capture her when I clearly had the chance and why had she let me go? These questions spun in my head as I made my way to the medical bay.

Bypassing the two exam beds in the middle of the room, I went straight to the shelves of equipment and supplies lining the walls. I found the sterilizing and cleansing solution and after spraying the cut, I rolled glue over it, sealing the wound and protecting it all at once. I rummaged through a drawer until I found a roll of gauze and wrapped that around the wound, too. It was a shallow cut and I had the feeling that she'd done that purposefully. A few inches deeper and she could've nicked my femoral artery and I would've bled out before I could even think of jumping back to my ship.

None of this made any sense. Why did she let me live?

Back on the bridge, I stood over the table studying the map of Valinor. I had to go back and try again.

"Hey boss," Briar said, tapping her long fingers on the table.

"What is it?" I asked without looking up.

"Anything else you want to tell us?"

"About?"

"What happened down there?" Briar Ladetto was our navigations expert, but she was by far the smartest person on our crew. She knew something about everything and if she didn't, she would hack any computer to figure it out.

Rolling my eyes, I said, "Nothing, Briar."

"That's bull," Huxley challenged.

"What's your problem?" I challenged.

"No problem. Just curious as to how a legendary warrior such as yourself didn't get the job done on the very first try. I mean, this might be a first."

"Are you trying to piss me off?" I growled.

He put up his hands and backed away, but kept the smirk on his face. "Nope."

"Concentrate on your jobs," I spat.

Frustrated, I took off to the weapons training room. Each of the walls was lined with weapons. Guns such as simple handguns to laser guns to grenade launchers hung on one wall. Swords of all sizes hung from the wall opposite the guns. The third wall consisted of a variety of weapons: fighting sticks, battle-axes, daggers, and bombs. I ran my fingers over the hilt of my favorite double-edged sword—a type of claymore with a jeweled cross-guard and grip. Turning from those, I grabbed a pair of hand wraps. This level of frustration required some impact. Not even a minute later, I'd worked up a good sweat while punching the heavy bag.

"Want someone to spar with?" Briar asked from the doorway.

The wound in my thigh hurt, but not so much that I would opt out of a good sparing match. Besides, I was agitated and I had to find a way to work off this energy so I could think straight. "Sure. Wrap up."

Briar pushed her pink hair back with a headband and wrapped her hands, securing the ends nice and tight before she turned to me and squared her stance. A thrill of anticipation, not unlike the one that had coursed through me when I faced off with the empress, rushed through my body. Briar and I were about the same size and weight and she was good at hand to hand. Just not as good as me.

We circled each other for a moment, shifted into combat stance, and then she came at me. We grappled for a few tense moments, each of us straining to throw the other to the floor, but eventually I got the best of her. I threw her down on her back, face up, and mimed a killing blow before I let her up.

"Go again?" I asked.

"Sure."

I held out my hand, offering to help her up. She took it hesitantly and I hauled her to her feet.

I took a step forward and threw a right cross. She sidestepped, twisted her body, brought her leg up, and kicked me in the stomach. Grabbing her foot, I pushed back hard, and she went flying. She had barely hit the ground before I pounced on her. Knees pinning her arms to the floor and sitting on her chest, I had her pinned in a position for another killing blow. I still had it. I could still do it. How in the world had the Empress gotten the better of me?

After the sparing session I went to my room and showered. Lying in bed attempting to sleep, the Empress' face kept appearing in my mind's eye. I flipped over and buried my head in the pillow, which only made it worse. I had to be honest with myself. The Empress had a weapon I had never encountered before. She was beautiful. Yes, I'd encountered beautiful women before, but I'd never been charged with kidnapping or killing them. But so what? Why did that matter? There were plenty of attractive people in the universe. Why had I let that affect me?

A low beep told me someone from the bridge was trying to contact me. "What is it?" I asked.

"Caspar is calling," Huxley said.

I cursed under my breath. "On my way."

The moment I stalked back into the room everyone's eyes were on me. "Put him onscreen."

The man who had destroyed my life appeared onscreen. When I was a kid, Caspar Regnier abducted my family along with almost a hundred others from our home. He dumped us on a planet that was barely survivable. Then, a couple years later, he took the kids from their parents—myself included—and raised us on his ship, training us to become the lethal warriors we were today. He gave us the ship and forced us to do things for him by threatening the lives of our families.

Caspar was twice my age, with a full head of black, spiked hair. His upper lip was perpetually curled up like he smelled something rotten, but that was how he always looked when we spoke. He hated the sight of me. "I don't like to be kept waiting, Everleigh."

I didn't respond. Didn't apologize. Nothing.

He pursed his lips. "Where is the Empress?"

"I'll have her soon."

"Soon? Why don't you have her yet?" he demanded.

"She's very protected."

His nostrils flared. "Do I need to remind you that I hold your family in the palm of my hand? I could crush them." He brought his hands together like he was smashing something in them. "Maybe they won't have any food to eat for a few days? Maybe a sickness will spread through the community?"

My hands balled into fists. "Let them be. You'll have her soon." I hit the end button and marched over to the map of Valinor.

Why did he need to have *her*? It didn't matter. I had to

get her and turn her over. I had to do it for my family. For the families of my crew.

"Do we know where she lives? Is there a castle?"

"There's no castle. We're not sure where she lives," Zabe stated. Zabrador "Zabe" Torpey was the fourth member of our crew. He was the mission specialist, took care of the Nirvana, and us.

"So actually jumping into her home won't work." I paced the floor. "I'll just go back again."

"She's not there," Briar reported.

"Not on Valinor? I just left there."

"She's heading to a summit meeting for Alliance members that's taking place tomorrow on Caipra. The leaders of twenty worlds will be there, Valinor included."

"A summit? What kind of summit? Were we invited?"

"No, Ever. Did you not hear her? It's a meeting for those in the Alliance. We neither have a home planet to rule nor are we part of the Alliance." Huxley rolled his eyes.

"You're lucky I like you or I'd lock you up for your sarcasm."

Huxley scoffed. "I appreciate your leniency."

I punched him on the shoulder. "Get us there. Use the cloaking device."

Grabbing her at the summit would be easier than trying to take her on her home planet. At most she would travel with a small detachment, but I could handle that. It was the Empress herself that had me worried. I tried not to think about her. Tried not to think of her hair and how it caught the light of their setting sunstar. Those bright, blue eyes of hers. The way my heart sped up when she had me pinned to the ground.

"What's on your mind, Ever?"

"Just plotting."

"Like the evil villain you are."

Laughing, I nodded, and picked up a deck of cards. "Dealer's choice."

I dealt a game of Loaded. Zabe and Briar sat down at the table to play, too. Hux passed around a bottle of Temptation, a colorless ninety-five proof alcohol.

Caipra, the planet they were meeting on, was discovered a hundred years ago. A battle took place between the warring occupants of the planet and destroyed so much of the land that only a few could live there now. Over time, Caipra became a sort of neutral zone for planetary meetings and discussions. A building was erected a few earthyears ago and became a neutral place for intergalactic meetings.

"I wonder what's going on down there."

"I could hack in," Briar offered.

A quick nod from me was all she needed before her hands were flying over the keyboard. A few minutes later, she smiled proudly.

"You're in?"

Huxley and I surveyed the room and took note of who was present from the video feed that Briar had patched us into. The conference room was a large and circular with a hallway that ran around it. Four corridors stemmed from it. Attached were a hotel, cafeteria, and lounge. The fourth corridor led to the docking bay.

"Any suggestions on the best way to do this?" I wished I could send one of the others, but this was my responsibility and I had never left a job incomplete.

"Lie in wait. When she's alone, grab her and jump back.

The only difference here is there's a lot of others around," Huxley said.

"They're announcing everyone," Briar said.

"Can you put it on speaker?"

With a tap of a button, a male voice filled the room as he read off names. "President Ava Debold of Naweth, King Hesh Sekoni of Tured, Empress Akacia Sparks of Valinor."

When he finally finished, they called the meeting to order. "The first item on our agenda is to welcome Queen Elodie Maas of Treasa. They have joined the Alliance." There was applause. "Queen Mass, please sign your name here."

Then began the most boring earthhour of my life. I didn't know how anyone could sit through meetings like these. People trading with each other, negotiating with one another, and discussing where the space pirates had last been seen.

"Empress Sparks."

My ears perked up at the sound of her name.

"I am Captain Reeve of The Authority. I'd like to ask you to reconsider your decision to let us have a station on Valinor. It would be very beneficial to us."

"I'm sure it would."

Hearing her voice made my heart beat faster.

"I'm sorry. I must stick with the original decision. Valinor was discovered by a privately owned spacecraft, as you know. My great-great-grandmother was the commander of that spacecraft. Valinor is not obligated to let you build there, nor do we want you to. We are a simple people and would like to keep it that way."

"Very well," Reeve replied. "We will respect your decision."

I snorted. "I'm sure they're fuming."

"I can't imagine they get turned down often," Briar added. "The empress has some guts."

That she did.

"Is there a schedule of events? I don't want to sit around and wait, but I can't exactly just jump in there and grab her."

Briar's eyes scanned the screen. "There's a break coming up."

"Alright. Stay cloaked. I'll be back as soon as possible." I centered myself in the jump circle and pressed the button.

Landing in a closet, I stepped around cleaning supplies and crept down to the meeting hall. I counted twenty world leaders in attendance sitting around a large, circular table from where I stood, a few that I detested, and wished I could grab instead of the Empress, but she was who Casper wanted.

My eyes searched the room and when my eyes land on her, my breath caught. She was even more beautiful in this setting. Her blonde hair was braided to the side. A small, delicate crown sat on her head. Those stunning blue eyes of hers were outlined in the same hue as the form-fitting, blue and silver outfit she wore. It seemed to be some sort of armor, but it was one that hugged her every dip, curve, and slope.

Stop thinking of her like that. She was a target. That's it. That's all.

I stayed hidden as the moderator announced the break and the leaders stood. Each had a guard that followed them. A few others approached the Empress. Her lips were pulled tight as if she couldn't wait to get out of there. Finally, she broke free and hurried out of the room. A tall, buff man followed close behind with his hand on the gun holstered on his side.

Outside the bathroom door, she turned to him. "Thank you, Dieter. Why don't you take a few minutes?"

"I'm supposed to guard you, Empress."

"I need to go to the bathroom. I'm sure you could use the break as well."

He gave a slight nod and they went their separate ways. But before I could go in after her, a few of the leaders walked past where I was hidden.

"This meeting is going to last for hours," one whined.

"At least we get breaks."

"When do you suppose the food will be served?"

As I waited, my eyes surveyed the area for the best way to grab her and go. She came out of the bathroom and walked over to a window. Motioning for her guard to return to the conference room, she stared out at the orange-red sky. Now was my chance. I slipped out of my hiding spot and walked toward her. She turned and our eyes met. Surprise and recognition flickered across her face, but before I could grab her, a loud explosion threw me backward. My head hit the wall and everything went black.

A burnt smell lingered in the air. Someone shook me and yelled things I couldn't understand. My head was pounding. Without opening my eyes, I slapped whoever it was away.

"Come on! We need to get out of here!"

I knew that voice, but getting my eyes to open was a problem.

"I can't carry you."

I forced my eyes open. Everything was blurry.

"Can you stand?" the voice asked.

I didn't know. My head hurt so much, I had no clue how the rest of my body was.

Hands pulled at me, helping me to my feet. Finally my body got with it and I was able to stand on my own.

I looked at the person who helped me. There she was with a slight smile on her face. Her crown was gone and her blonde curls were streaked with red—wait. That was blood. Did she have a head wound? Was she hurt? And how did she manage to make that look sexy? Oh, God. There I went again with the whole sexy thing.

"Let's go." She started walking and I hobbled after her.

Pain shot through my body. "Ah!"

"What is it?" the empress asked.

I pulled up my shirt. Something was sticking out of my side. Metal of some sort, from whatever had blown up.

"Shit," she swore, examining the wound.

Another explosion—smaller this time—came from down the corridor. "Can you keep going? We have to go."

"Yes." I would push through the pain. I had no choice.

As quick as we could, we hurried down the hall.

"What happened?" I asked.

"An attack."

"I got that much. Do you know who? Or why?"

"No. It came out of nowhere."

"How many are down?"

"Most? All? I don't know. We can talk later. Right now we have to get to my ship." Just as the words came out of her mouth, more explosions went off and her face went ghostly pale.

Following her gaze, I realized the urgency of the situation we were in. The ships were blowing up—one by one.

There were shouts coming from behind us. I didn't know if they were friend or foe. We needed to get out of there. I glanced at the Empress and saw a few tears slide down her face, though she didn't make a sound.

"We've got to go," I agreed and we got moving again.

"Where are we going to go?" she asked turning to me. "All the ships have been destroyed."

"Not mine. It's cloaked." I took the jump device out of my pocket and opened it up. An immediate connection was found—indicated by a dim blue light—verifying that my ship was still there and functioning. "Ready?"

She looked at me, vulnerable and excited. "Okay."

I grabbed her hand, ignoring the way goose bumps covered every inch of me when our palms touched, and pressed the button.

Seconds later, we were in my ship.

There were lights blinking and noises screaming. All three of my crewmembers turned to me.

"You got the Empress," Huxley said, quickly shutting up when I shot him a look.

"Ever! Our ship has been damaged—" Zabe reported.

"Were we hit?"

"Not directly. The force of the explosions and maybe some debris."

"How badly?" I asked.

"We can't FTL."

"Can we move at all?" My body felt like it was on fire. The edges of my vision were dark and blurry.

"Yes."

"Then get us out of here," I gave the order and then collapsed on the ground.

"Ever!" Huxley shouted and knelt by my side.

"She has a wound from the explosion. Do you have a doctor?" the Empress asked.

"No."

"Medical bay?"

"Yes."

"Help me get her there."

Huxley scooped me up and hurried down the corridor to the med bay. Carefully, he placed me on the table. The Empress pulled up my shirt again and examined the wound. "It moved. I can take it out. Laser wand?"

"Shit! Ours is broken," Huxley exclaimed.

"Suture kit?"

"Yes."

"Do you have any anesthesia?"

"Just do it. I can handle it," I said.

"Put this in your mouth," she said, shoving in a piece of cloth. "Bite down on it to keep from screaming."

I squeezed my eyes shut and waited.

The second she touched the metal shard pain shot through my body. She yanked it out then applied pressure to stop the bleeding. My vision swam. I wasn't going to stay conscious through this. Sharp pricks came next as she stitched me up. That's when I let the darkness come. It surrounded me and I felt nothing.

CHAPTER THREE

AKACIA

AFTER AN HOUR OF PACING the room, I finally sat down in a chair. The guy who had carried her—Ever, that's what they called her—had offered to bring me to a room, but I refused. "You won't be able to leave this room without one of us. The door will be locked. You understand? We don't know you." He had been called back to the bridge, but before he left, he patted me down, looking for weapons, but I had none. They weren't allowed on Caipra. "The computer sees everything on this ship. Zia, lock the supplies."

I could hear locks engaging all over the room. "I won't hurt her. I just saved her."

"Are you sure you wouldn't be more comfortable in a room?" He had green eyes and silver hair, which was odd because he seemed way too young to have gone completely gray.

"No." I couldn't leave her. I should. I had heard what they said on the bridge. They were happy I was with her. She had been sent to capture me and that should have me worried, but that wasn't the thought that was foremost in my mind.

Who attacked Caipra? Were there survivors? Would they realize I was missing? My spacecraft was gone, which meant my crew was gone. Silent tears ran down my face as I thought of each of them and their families. Had they received the news back home? If they had, they would send out a unit to rescue me. But what if…what if they thought I was dead?

My eyes wandered and landed on her face. She had a black eye and an angry, purple bruise on her cheek. Neither took away from her striking features. Her hair had fallen away from her ears showing the earrings that ran from her lobes to both sides of her helix. Her full lips were slightly parted. She looked peaceful just lying there, but something told me peaceful wasn't a word anyone would use to describe her. Seconds later, I knew exactly why.

Without so much as a gasp she sat up with a wild look in her eyes and looked around the room frantically. I stayed in the chair watching as she looked around and then down at her wound. Finally her golden eyes found mine.

"Empress."

"I'm here," I answered, going to her side. "It's good you're awake. Are you in any pain?"

Her eyes searched mine, like she was looking for an answer for a question that I didn't ask. She shook her head. A slight grimace on her face was the only sign she was in pain. "You fixed me."

"Your injuries weren't that bad."

"Thanks."

"You can thank me by returning me to my planet," was my firm response.

"I saved your life, too. Shouldn't we be even?"

She was right, though I wasn't giving in. I just needed some time to figure out how to get back home. "I am the Empress.

My people depend on me. Can I at least call and tell them I'm alive?"

"Fine, but you cannot tell them where you are."

"And where am I?"

She held my eyes. "The Nirvana."

I knew the name, Nirvana. It was a ship of criminals that were wanted by the Authority for a long list of crimes including stealing and murder. I swallowed hard. What in the universe did the Nirvana want with me? My heart pounded and I took deep breaths to calm myself down. Don't show fear. Get word to Valinor. Bristow can figure out where I am. "Your reputation precedes you."

"Then you know just how lethal we are." She shifted like she was uncomfortable. "Let's get to the bridge."

"You should rest." I didn't know why I was still concerned about her wellbeing, but I was.

"I'm fine."

The door to the bridge opened as she approached. Three pairs of curious eyes awaited us on the other side. There were two males and a female. One was the guy who helped me with Ever earlier. The other had darker skin and dark eyes. The girl looked younger than all of them. A headband kept her short pink hair out of her blue eyes. Although different colors, their eyes were all the same. I couldn't explain how. Different. Deep. Soulful. Tortured.

Ever's voice brought me back to the present. "I'm fine, guys. Really. Can we open a channel to Valinor? The Empress needs to get word to her family that she's alive."

"Yes." The girl waved me to her. "I'm Briar. Zia, please hail the planet, Valinor."

"We need to talk, Everleigh." The green-eyed guy grabbed

her arm and dragged her to a corner. I could tell by their facial expressions that it wasn't a warm and fuzzy, "glad you're okay," kind of discussion. But I couldn't focus on that too much because we'd made contact with Valinor.

"Empress? Akacia?" It was Galton's voice.

"Galton. I'm okay. I was rescued."

"Were you hurt?" Vika asked.

"No. The Razor though. It was destroyed with everyone on board. I'm not sure about Dieter. I assume he's gone."

"He is." Galton was silent for a minute. "It is a great loss. We will have a service as soon as you return. Do you know when that'll be?"

An outburst from Everleigh grabbed my attention. "This is my ship! I am the commander!" She pulled away from them.

"Empress?" Galton questioned.

Turning back to the screen I asked, "Do you know what happened?"

Vika answered, "An attack from Wapi. Trying to break up alliances again."

"Bugger me. How many were killed?"

"Besides you, only two remain alive. Where are you, Empress? We'll send someone for you."

"We'll get her home," Ever interrupted and I shot her a questioning look.

"Very well. To whom do we owe the thank you?"

"None needed," she said.

Bristow rushed into view. "Kaci! I'm so glad you weren't harmed."

"Bristow, it's beautiful up here. I wish you were here with me." I crossed my arms in front of my body, but instead of resting all the fingers of my right hand on my upper left arm,

I tucked away all but two. Then I tapped those fingers on my upper arm twice. It was a signal Bristow and I had used as kids when we wanted the other to save us from a boring lecture or being cooped up.

He nodded. "Maybe soon."

"Fare thee well."

"Fare thee well, Empress."

Everleigh hit the end button and turned to look at me. There was something in her eyes that said she was quite pleased with her "catch," meaning me.

I needed to make nice with these people. Not let on that I was even a tiny bit afraid. "You're called Everleigh," I stated, guessing Ever was a nickname her friends used. When she didn't answer, I added, "You know who I am."

"You're the Empress."

"Akacia. My name is Akacia. Figured we should be on first name terms since you keep trying to kidnap me."

One corner of her mouth twitched like she wanted to smile. "Everleigh."

"You went to the meeting to capture me?"

"Yes," she confirmed.

"Why is it you want me?"

"I don't."

I was confused for a minute and then it hit me. "Someone else does. Someone hired you?"

"Yes."

"Who?"

"Caspar Regnier."

Another well-known criminal. Caspar was even on the most wanted list. "Why would he want me?"

She didn't answer.

"Are you really going to take me home?"

"I'd like to."

It was a strange reply. I waited for the rest of the answer, but it didn't come. She wasn't going to explain. Looking around at the others in the room, I stated the obvious, "They're upset with you."

She shrugged. Both the males looked as if they'd like to tear me limb from limb. Their job was to capture me. Even if Everleigh agreed to take me home, would they allow it? I should be open with them, make them like me. Maybe if they got to know me, they wouldn't turn me over. I could give them the money they had been expecting from the job.

"I'm Akacia," I said, sticking out my hand to shake theirs.

"Huxley," the green-eyed one with the silver hair said. When the other didn't answer, Huxley offered his name. "That's Zabe."

"Nice to meet you. Thank you for helping me."

Zabe growled and stormed off. Huxley and Briar turned away, directing their attention back to their jobs. Well, it was a start. I had to keep trying.

"How long until we reach Valinor?" I asked.

"FTL is down. We need to stop and have it fixed. There's a station a few days away at top speed," Huxley answered.

Everleigh nodded and Briar said, "Zia, plot course to Gledi Station."

"Done. Would you like me to set up any appointments for you, Briar?" the computer answered in a calm voice.

"One to repair the ship and order a laser wand along with any supplies we need."

"Nothing fun?" the computer's voice rose a bit like she was curious.

"Not this time."

"Very well."

"That's your computer?" I asked.

"Yes. She is very human-like," Everleigh said. I didn't miss the smile she sent Briar's way. Her pink-haired shipmate must have been the one who programmed it.

"Let me show you to your room," Everleigh offered, tucking her long hair behind her ear.

"Can I ask you something?"

She nodded.

"The attack. You didn't have anything to do with that... did you?" We turned a corner and made our way down a long, narrow corridor.

"No! I am a thief. I steal things. I am not a murderer." There was a hesitation in her voice.

"Are you sure?"

Her lips tightened into a thin, grim line. "I've only killed because my life was in danger," she said.

"So you're not a coldblooded murderer, but you are a killer."

Everleigh shot me a look that dared me to say more. "I suppose you're right."

"Will you kill me?"

Very quietly, she answered, "No. Not you."

"You threatened to."

She was quiet for a moment. Maybe trying to remember the conversation I was talking about. "Yes, but I won't."

The way she said it, with a tiny bit of tenderness, warmed my heart. A strange reaction considering that she was my captor. We stopped and she pressed her hand on a pad. A door slid open revealing a small bedroom.

"Not a cell?" I asked.

She ignored the comment. "There's a bathroom through that door. Has a shower."

I bit my lip. "I could use one."

She lingered in the door, watching me, almost like she didn't want to go. Truth be told, I didn't want her to. Her eyes moved rapidly over my body, lingering here and there. The way she looked at me—like I was the most beautiful thing she's ever seen—brought heat to my cheeks.

A minute later, her expression changed, like she snapped back to reality. She gave me a curt nod and slipped out the door.

It was like the room dimmed and turned colder without her there. I wanted to call after her, ask her to sit with me, talk a while, but instead I sighed and sat on the bed. I kicked off my shoes and then went to the bathroom. Suddenly I couldn't get out of my clothes fast enough. I ripped them off my body and jumped in the shower. The hot water mixed with my tears and rinsed off the dirt and blood.

I had almost died today in an explosion—no, an attack. There were people out there who wanted us dead. If the Wapi found out some of us were still alive, would they try again? I shook my head. I couldn't worry about that right now. For now, my heart still beat and air still filled my lungs. I was okay.

My dirty, ripped clothes were in a pile behind the bathroom door. I didn't want to put them on again. Back in the room, I found a stack of clothes folded neatly on the bed. The faded T-shirt and loose fitting pants were soft and comfortable. I wondered if Everleigh herself had dropped them off or she had someone else do it. I decided it didn't matter. I was happy to have them.

Exhaustion hit quickly and I crawled into the large bed. I was out before my head hit the pillow.

When I woke, my stomach was rumbling. A loud, almost painful growling. I rolled out of bed, cleaned up in the bathroom, and opened the door. Looking both ways, I tried to remember which way we had come last night.

"Empress."

I jumped and turned in the direction of the voice. Everleigh stood there, dressed in tight, black pants and a long-sleeve half shirt that showed off her belly button. All decency left me as I took in the sight of her. Every part of her was delicious. From her long neck to her supple breasts to the bit of skin showing at her midriff. She wore two leg holsters; one held a gun and the other held a knife. Could I trust her word? Would she kill me if she were forced to do it?

Everleigh closed the space between us, the air felt like it was on fire. My heart thumped in my chest. Licking my lips, I drew in a calming breath and let it out in a slow sigh.

"Call me Akacia…or Kaci. My friends call me Kaci."

"Am I a friend?"

I bit my lip to tame my smile. "You got me off that planet. Saved my life. That makes you a friend."

A smile pulled at the corners of her mouth, a sad smile. I wanted to ask what was wrong, but she turned abruptly and waved for me to follow her.

"Thank you," I said to her back as we made our way down the narrow corridor again.

"For?"

"The clothes."

She nodded. "Figured you wouldn't want to put those dirty clothes back on."

The corridor led to a kitchen. Everleigh opened some cabinets. "See anything you think you would like?"

"Is that cereal?"

Another nod. "Sit."

"I can get it myself."

"Just sit."

I sat down and she placed a bowl and a spoon in front of me then went back for the box of cereal and milk. She picked up the box and poured the cereal into the bowl. When she put her hand around the jug of milk, I reached out and put my hand on hers. Her breath caught in her throat. Was that a reaction to my touch?

"I may be an Empress, but I can pour my own milk."

Everleigh nodded again and withdrew her hand. I poured the milk and started eating. She sat across from me, her hands folded and resting on the table.

"Aren't you going to eat?"

"I was up early. I ate then."

In between bites, I said, "Breakfast at home would be fruit and breads. I haven't had cereal in a long time."

She smiled again, but kept quiet.

"What do you like?" I asked. It was awkward to have someone watch me slurp cereal. Small talk was, too, but it was infinitely better than wondering if I had milk dribbling down my chin after every mouthful.

"Eggs. I like the way Huxley makes them."

"I'd like to try them."

"Next time I'll ask him to make some."

I finished the cereal and then asked, "So, are you going to give me a tour?"

"Would you like one?"

"Yes."

"Okay." She stood up, put my dishes in the sink, and waited for me to follow.

She showed me around the different rooms; mechanical, lounge, weapons training, and then led me into a large observation room with windows so big and clear, it felt like I was actually outside rather than in a spacecraft. "You've seen the bridge and kitchen. Not much else, but the crew's rooms."

"And yours," I said, softly.

Everleigh's eyes widened for a few seconds then she turned and started walking. I wasn't sure if she was taking me somewhere else or to her room until she stopped in front of her door and put her hand on the pad. The door slid open and she stepped aside to let me go in first.

A large bed sat in the middle of the room covered in fluffy pillows and warm looking blankets. There was a good size wardrobe and a desk with a computer screen wall. There weren't any pictures or anything really personal out in the open, except for the ceiling. That had to be personal. It was a painting of beautiful wild animals in a forest.

"Wow."

She stood next to me. "Gives me something to look at. I don't have any windows."

"It's beautiful."

Her shoulder brushed against mine and every inch of my skin reacted as if she'd touched me intentionally. *Think of something to ask. Think of something to say. Just do something.*

"Where's your planet?" I asked.

"I don't have one."

Her fingers brushed against mine. Now that was intentional. I looked at her and found that she was staring at me. My stomach did a lazy flip like it had that first time I'd jumped from one place to another. The air grew thick as my gaze traveled down to her lips and back up to her eyes. I tangled my fingers in hers, wanting to pull her closer, but afraid to make the first move. Everleigh swallowed and her mouth opened then closed again as though she was holding back words she wanted to say. After a minute, she broke our gaze and stepped away and the miniscule space she'd made between our bodies made me feel cold.

"So what now?"

"I have some work to do," she replied.

"Is it strenuous?"

"What?"

"Your work?"

"No."

"Good. You should still rest. Your body needs to heal. In fact, I should probably check the stitches."

"Later." She said then gestured for me to follow her out of her room.

"You said you steal things. Is that what all four of you do?"

She narrowed her eyes like she thought it might be a trick question, but then she nodded. "We're a team."

Raised voices greeted us as we approached the bridge. When the door opened, they stopped abruptly and stared at us. I must have been the topic of their disagreement and I could guess why.

Smile, I reminded myself. "Good morning! You have an awesome spacecraft. And Huxley, I hear you make eggs. I would love to try them."

Huxley looked confused, but he nodded. "Sure."

"She shouldn't be here, Everleigh," the one named Zabe blurted, his voice gruff.

"And where should she be?" Everleigh asked, her voice calm and even.

"She's a target. She should be locked up," he said as he glared at me.

"We're not locking her up. She saved my life."

"Hardly."

"What's that supposed to mean?" she asked.

"You've had worse injuries. You're playing with fire, Ever."

"I promise you I'm not a threat," I said, attempting to reassure him—to reassure all of them.

"It's not you I'm worried about, Empress," he said. He spat out my title like it was a dirty word. "Nor is it our place to decide. We were sent to acquire you and--"

"Enough!" Everleigh growled and went to her control center. Zabe kicked a chair across the room and stormed off.

The silence that followed his exit was awkward. I walked to the window and stared into the great dark. Thinking back to my conversations with Bristow and how we wanted to explore. He'd be very jealous right now. Well, except for the fact that I wasn't on an adventure. Not really. Zabe had just made it clear that I was meant to be a prisoner. How long before Everleigh agreed? She was their commander and of course they would follow her orders, but…people did bad things for money.

"Everything okay, Empress?" Briar asked, coming to stand beside me at the window.

"Just Akacia." I was never one for formal titles and Empress always felt like too big of a title for me. Besides I was trying to get these guys to like me. "I'm fine. Thanks."

"Did you sleep well?"

44

"I did."

"I have found news regarding the attack on Caipra," Zia, the computer, interrupted.

Briar returned to the computer. "Go ahead."

"The news reports say there were two Wapi spacecrafts involved. The Authority destroyed one. They're in pursuit of the other," Zia continued.

"See what the public knows about what happened at Caipra," Everleigh said and soon they were all lost in research and talking.

With everyone busy, I found myself wandering around the spacecraft. Soon I arrived at the training room. There was an array of weapons. I knew many of them, but there were still quite a bit I didn't recognize. I admired a black prince dagger with a leather wrapped handle. My eyes traveled around the room amazed at the collection. These weapons were impressive and dangerous and if all of them were as skilled as Everleigh, I stood no chance against them.

I picked up a rapier and swung it around for a minute. It didn't feel right in my hands so I put it back and grabbed a sabre, but that wasn't really my style either. One of the swords further down caught my eye—a broadsword—and I picked it up and gave it a few swings to see how it felt in my hands.

"Want to spar?"

I spun around to find Everleigh standing there with a smile playing on her lips that was somewhere between a flirt and a challenge. "Sure."

She picked up a claymore and we stood a few feet apart in the middle of the room. Circling with swords up, I studied the way she moved. She seemed relaxed. Too relaxed. Was she underestimating my skill? I struck first, taking a looping swing that she blocked with little effort. We did that for a while, trading blows back and forth, striking and blocking. It didn't seem to be going anywhere, so I leveled a stronger, more deliberate, blow at her chest and she barely evaded with a quick jump backward. Before she had time to renew her attack, I delivered a series of strikes that whooshed near her head.

Her lips widened into a sexy sneer and then she sprang at me, delivering a vicious and unrelenting attack, forcing me backward. Her blows were fast and solid, and she kept at it until she whacked the sword out of my hand.

I held up my hands, giving up. "You win." She was good, perhaps better than me. This was nothing like sparring with Bristow. I realize now that he may have gone a bit easy on me.

Everleigh smiled and lowered her sword. "You're good."

"We should do that again. It's been a long time since—"

"You're bleeding," Everleigh interrupted, grabbing my arms alternately, searching for cuts. .

"It's not me. It's you. Your stitches."

"Oh." Relief flooded her face.

"We shouldn't have been sparring with your injury. I'm sorry. I forgot."

"It's fine. It doesn't hurt."

"Let's go fix it."

She gave a small nod and led me to the med bay. I pointed to the table and she let out a little sigh and then climbed on.

"Lay down."

She huffed and lay on her back as I searched for all the supplies I needed. Turning back to her, I swallowed hard as I pulled her shirt up just enough to examine the wound. My fingers grazed her skin and a gasp escaped her lips. The bandage was soaked with blood. I peeled it off carefully, but quickly.

Using some damp gauze, I cleaned the cut, sprayed a numbing spray, and then stitched her back up. A quick smear of ointment to aid in healing and keep it from getting infected went on before I applied a new bandage.

"Looks good. Don't overdo it," I said, pulling her shirt back down. I took a few more steps back and watched as she stood up.

"Thanks."

For the next couple earthdays, I let myself get close enough for them to warm up to me a little. I could tell it was working, at least with three of them.

Briar and I were standing shoulder to shoulder while she studied maps of different galaxies.

Curiously, I inquired, "Are you looking for something in particular?"

The others looked at her. Their glares were almost cautionary. "No," she answered. "Just fun places to explore."

I knew it was a lie, but now wasn't the time for me to push. "Have you guys been to many planets?"

This seemed to get Briar and Huxley to open up. They talked about many of the places they had been and shared some of the places they still had to see. Everleigh would even jump in here and there, her face lighting up when she spoke of the places she still wanted to visit. As usual, Zabe stayed quiet. I was beginning to wonder if the scowl on his face was permanent. He wanted nothing to do with me.

"I have a call to make. You can stay with the crew," Ever said something to Huxley, who in turn nodded.

He walked over to where I was seated and asked, "Know how to play Loaded?"

Smiling, I responded, "Yes."

He waved over Zabe and Briar. Zabe came reluctantly and as they sat down, I realized they all had the same arrow tattoo on their necks. One just like Ever's. The four of us played a few hands of cards. I was good at this game and apparently that threw Zabe for a loop because he was used to winning. Huxley laughed at the even bigger scowl Zabe now had on his face when I won my third hand.

Huxley slapped Zabe on the back. "We finally found someone you can't beat."

"Don't jinx my luck," I teased. "How long have you guys been part of Everleigh's crew?"

"Couple of years, but I've known Ever for a long time," Huxley replied, dealing another hand.

"And you two?"

"We've all been together since the crew started," Briar said. "I didn't know her before."

"Me either," Zabe said. "But we're all family now."

"You all have the same tattoo on your neck," I stated. "What does it mean?"

"Where there's a will, there's a way," Huxley replied. "But it does show that we're part of the same crew."

"Everleigh has another symbol next to hers."

"It means chief. It marks her as the leader of our crew."

"What is she like?"

"She's the best," Briar responded.

I wanted to know everything I could about her. "She seems so guarded."

The three of them nodded, but said nothing more. It was clear I wasn't going to get any information out of them. They were loyal to Ever and any answer would be a betrayal.

CHAPTER FOUR

EVERLEIGH

I stood in the doorway, watching Akacia play a game with Zabe and Briar. Strange, but having her here made my crew feel complete. The crew and I had been a family of sorts from day one, but I always felt like something was missing. This was it. But all of that was complicated by the fact that she was a target to be delivered to Caspar. Akacia wasn't part of our family. She never could be.

"She's squizz," Huxley said, walking up next to me.

I nodded.

"I see the way you look at her, Ever."

I shot him a sideways glance.

"We can't keep her."

I choked back a laugh. "She's not a puppy, Hux."

"She most certainly is not, but you know what I mean. We have to finish the job."

"Tell me how," I demanded through my teeth. "How do I just turn her over to that evil bastard?"

"We've done it plenty of times."

"Not with *her*." My eyes burned with unshed tears. "I have to find a way out of this."

Later that night, after Akacia had gone to bed, the four of us convened on the bridge. Unable to come up with a solution of my own, I did the only thing that made sense—sat down with my crew to find a way around it.

"I can't hand her over to Caspar. The attack on Caipra bought us some time. Zia told us the Authority hasn't confirmed how many were killed or released any names yet. I insinuated to Caspar that she could be one of them."

I knew my crew was looking at me like I had lost my mind as I paced the bridge muttering ideas. "What if we just took off? Went somewhere nobody could find us?"

"So you're going to abduct the Empress, never return her, and we're all going to vanish into the great unknown?" Zabe said.

"Sure."

He arched an eyebrow. "You're not thinking clearly."

"Why couldn't we?"

"She might have a problem with that, for one. And you really think Caspar is going to let us disappear?" Huxley furrowed his brow.

"What if he takes it out on our families?" Briar asked.

"Then we take him out."

"You want to kill him? Is she that important to you? You don't even know her!" Zabe exclaimed.

"We'll fix the FTL drive and vanish until we can come up with a plan to kill him. As long as Caspar doesn't know we have her, we have time."

"How long do you really think he's going to give us? He's already mad he doesn't have her yet," Briar was the voice of reason. It wouldn't take him long.

"Maybe a couple of days. That should be enough time to come up with a plan."

"Ever, you have to think about the big picture here." Huxley reached out to me.

I put up my hand to stop him from saying anything more. "Come up with more options then." I said, then I left the bridge and retired to my quarters.

In the morning, the conversation I had with my crew last night weighed heavy on my mind as I made my way to Kaci's room to tell her breakfast would be ready soon. Would she want to stay with us? Outside her door, I hit the button to signal to her I was there.

Instead of just answering the intercom, she opened the door still wearing the cami and shorts she slept in. My heart rate accelerated.

"Hi."

"What's up?" she asked, smiling brightly.

Her smile made me feel weird inside. Tingly. Warm. "Eggs," I blurted then cleared my throat. "I just wanted to let you know the eggs are almost done if you want to have some."

"I'll just get changed. Do you want to come in or…"

"I'll wait for you here."

She nodded and the door closed. I paced back and forth while I waited for her. What was I doing? Was I really considering giving up my life for someone I didn't know? What if she didn't share my feelings? What if she laughed in my face when I told her everything?

The door opened and she stepped out. "Ready."

Wordlessly, I led her to the kitchen. We plopped down on opposite sides of the table.

Huxley filled our plates with eggs. "Eat up!"

Akacia picked up her fork and dug into the food. Her face lit up as she chewed it and swallowed. "Oh damn, this is so good."

"Thanks, Empress."

"Akacia," she corrected him.

She didn't tell him to call her Kaci like she had with me. I found satisfaction in that bit of intimacy. I watched Kaci as she enjoyed each bite of eggs. Her expressions made me smile.

"We'll be docking at the station in a couple of hours. Do you want to go out and explore while the ship gets fixed?"

Her brow furrowed. "How do you do that? Aren't you like...wanted?"

A smile stretched across my face. "Money goes a long way. There are certain stations we can't go to. There are others that like a little extra money."

"Okay, then. I'd love to go out with y—" Her cheeks blushed something fierce. It was the cutest damn thing. "To go exploring."

I turned before she could see the blush in my own cheeks and cleaned up our plates. Briar was grinning at me from across the room.

"Do I look okay?" she asked innocently.

It was a simple question, but one that required me to look at her again. Her only clothing was the protective suit she wore to the summit meeting and that was a mess. She had been wearing my pants and T-shirt since. "I can give you another shirt."

"Okay. Thanks."

Briar's expression faded and she lifted the tablet that

she held and tapped on the glass. "We have a problem," she announced, meeting my eyes.

"What?"

"My source at the Authority says Valinor contacted them claiming we have abducted the Empress."

"They must have figured out who we were."

The look on Akacia's face said it all. "It's my fault. I sent Bristow a signal that I needed help when we talked. I didn't know what to think then. I was worried about what might happen to me. I'm sorry."

I searched her eyes and read her body language. She was being genuine. "There's nothing we can do about it now. Make sure our Gledi contact gets a bonus."

We walked in silence back to my room. When the door closed, she said, "I really am sorry."

I fingered a button on my pants. "I know."

"I'll make it right."

I almost laughed. "It's just another charge on our criminal log."

"Still, I'll fix it."

Something in me told me she would. She'd at least try. We would have to be extra careful at the space station.

The ship shuddered slightly as it docked. I pulled a shirt out of my drawer and handed it to Kaci.

"Do you have any clothes that aren't black?" she teased.

I shook my head. "No."

She slipped in the bathroom and when she came back out, she had my shirt on. I sucked in a breath. Her breasts were bigger than mine so the shirt was pulled tight across the chest.

"Does it look okay?"

I nodded, but took a step toward her and pulled up the middle a bit. "There are some people who aren't very nice."

"I can hold my own."

"I know. Turn around."

She turned—not even asking why. I stepped closer and gently pulled her hair out of the clip that held it up. A whiff of something sweet tickled my nose. I breathed in deeply. Honey. She smelled like honey and...milk. My heart pounded wildly. Her neck looked so soft, so smooth, so beautiful. I swallowed hard and moved her hair to cover her marking. "Don't want your marking to show."

She cleared her throat and said, "Thank you."

Kaci turned and our eyes met. The air between us crackled with electricity. Thoughts of kissing her filled my mind and I was just about to give in when Briar's voice came over the intercom.

"Ever? We're docked."

Swallowing hard, I answered, "Be right there."

A few minutes later, I led everyone, except Briar, out of the Nirvana and into the station. We always left one person behind to make sure nobody messed with the ship and everything ran smoothly. Briar stayed this time to monitor what was going on with the Authority.

"Everleigh!" a familiar voice called out.

"Hey, Jago."

"What happened to your ship?" the blond-haired man asked.

"FTL's broken. How fast can you get her fixed up?"

"Few earthhours." He wiped his dirty hands on his pants.

"Perfect. We sent ahead an order. If you need anything, Briar is on board."

"Got it."

When we got to the end of the corridor, I faced Zabe, Huxley, and Akacia. "Safe journeys."

Zabe let out a whoop before taking off. Huxley grinned and went in the other direction.

"What do you usually do here?" Akacia asked.

"Drink," I answered honestly. "Shop. Get a massage."

"Well, which do you want to do now?"

What I wanted to do and what I would do were totally different. "We could walk around and then eat somewhere."

She nodded, but then frowned. "I don't have any money."

"Don't worry. I do," I said.

Akacia's mouth fell open as we entered the main hall. It was dark even with the lights that recreated the light from a sunstar. The corridors and shops had no windows. We walked down the wide hallway full of people, past stores, clubs, casinos, and any service ever thought of. It was loud with voices and sounds echoing off the metallic walls.

"This is amazing." Her blue eyes were lit with wonder as we walked through the space station.

"Don't you ever get to go to the stations?"

"No. I've only been off Valinor a handful of times."

"Why?"

"Hidden as a child. When I turned sixteen, they let me out of hiding and I took my place. They didn't let me leave the planet for another two years. Then they accompanied me for the next year. Now I finally get to go to the meetings myself. Always with a crew, and a guard, never for long…" She sighed. "Bristow and I always dreamt of going exploring as kids, but when I grew up, I realized I couldn't go. I had to take care of my people and protect my planet."

I tried to see it the way she was seeing it for the first time. There were a lot of people and some of their clothing or hairstyles were more than interesting. While many people lived and worked at the station, most people were just passing through. All of the facilities were open around the clock because travelers arrived constantly.

The clothing people wore ranged from almost naked to glowing, full-length dresses to fancy tech outfits. We passed people dressed in long robes and wildly styled hair. Another group of people with tattoos covering the right side of their faces walked by.

"Their makeup is astounding," she said, gesturing to a group of people coming out of a clothing store wearing makeup that made them look like they had masks on.

I turned into the restaurant. "Two," I said to the hostess, who was an AI, but I doubted Akacia noticed. She was very human looking and could only be identified by a logo under her ear.

The hostess nodded and led us to a small table. We sat down and I touched the tabletop to pull up the menu. Akacia strained her neck to see what I was doing.

"Never seen one of these before either?"

Her cheeks burned red. "There are plenty of touchscreens in my command center and on my spacecraft—well there were, but I've never been to a restaurant."

"Really?"

"I'm the Empress. I have a chef." She rubbed her fingers over a simple, yet beautiful tattoo on her arm.

"Of course, you do," I said with a laugh. I swallowed and then took a few deep breaths to get up the courage to ask her a question. "Bristow? Is he your boyfriend?"

She met my eyes with a furrowed brow. "No. He's my best friend."

My heart beat faster hearing her answer and I thought about all the crazy feelings I've had since I first met her. Did she feel them, too?

"Do you dance?" she asked, looking at the people on the dance floor.

"Only after a few drinks." I didn't dance often. It wasn't something I enjoyed. Maybe it would be different with the right person.

"I'd like a drink. I don't get to do that either."

We both ordered mixed drinks and a few appetizers to share.

"Have you ever been to Earth?" she asked.

"No. It's something I'd like to do someday. I'm a bit of a history buff and I'd like to see it for myself. So much of the planet was destroyed, but there is still a lot I'd like to explore."

"It would be neat to see it all with my own eyes, not just in pictures or videos. It blows my mind when I read about how our ancestors thought Earth was the only habitable planet. Out of all the planets in the universe, they thought theirs was the only one."

"Right? What were they thinking?"

She took a sip of her drink. "Do you like watching movies?"

"When I'm in the mood. I like really old stuff from the early days on Earth and some of their first space exploration movies."

"Ah, yes. Some of the classics are the best films. Every once in a while, I'll watch one of the meaningless reality shows. I like to laugh."

Her laugh was perfect. Maybe I should get something funny for us to watch so I could hear that laugh again.

After we ate, we wandered the station. I loved watching her eyes fill with fascination as passed store windows.

"Wow. There are so many different fashions. Nearly every store is different."

"Let me guess. You have a seamstress, too."

She nodded. "Yes, but she's never made me anything like this." She gestured to my clothes on her body. "This is...sexy. I never have sexy clothes."

I couldn't help but laugh. Biting my lip, I decided to let go and have a little fun. I grabbed her and pulled her into one of the clothing stores.

We rummaged through the racks holding out clothes to each other. She looked at one dress with a slight smile on her face.

"You like that one?" I asked.

"Yes."

"Let's gather a bunch of things to just try on."

She looked at me like I was crazy. "Why?"

"Just because we can." I picked up a bright red, one-piece outfit. "Can you see me in this?"

She giggled. "No."

"Then it's the perfect thing to try on."

She chewed on her lip, but then nodded. "What the hell?" She started collecting random outfits from all over the store and then we headed toward the changing rooms.

"How about this one?" Akacia asked a few minutes later as she twirled around in a shiny fuchsia dress just outside the dressing room.

I burst out laughing. She looked like a giant flower.

"It's nice to see you smile."

Her remark caught me off guard and I ducked into my

dressing room. I wondered if her skin tingled when we touched like mine did. I stepped into a pair of tiered gypsy pants and slipped on a romantic, bohemian shirt with beaded details and old lace.

We opened the doors at the same time and came face-to-face. She had also put on a vintage mauve and dusty pink bohemian dress. While I had a good laugh at how the style looked on me, she looked absolutely stunning in her dress.

Soon we were laughing like old friends. We both tried on things neither of us would be caught dead in and maybe a few that we really did like. She was in awe of the skin tight, one-piece outfits that turned different colors with a touch.

"Oh, bugger!" she muttered from her dressing room.

"What?"

"I'm stuck." She giggled. "I'm going to find the sales lady to help."

"No! I'll help. Open your door."

A few seconds passed before I heard the lock click. She opened the door and I walked in and locked it behind me.

"Zipper's stuck." She moved her hair so I could see.

I struggled with the zipper for a minute before working it loose. I pulled it down exposing the intricate tattoos down her back. "Wow…"

Pink flamed her cheeks. "Phases of our moon, Oro."

I trailed my fingers down her back and she shuddered. It took everything in me not to lean in and kiss her. Our eyes met in the mirror. Her blue eyes were wide with curiosity and bright with anticipation. She tilted her head to the side just enough to expose the long line of her neck and that made my heart speed out of control. I closed the small space between us and let my lips touch her skin. Her breath hitched. She was so warm, so soft, and so perfect.

My lips trailed soft kisses up to her ear, she trembled and let out a low moan. I circled her waist with one arm to steady her. My heart felt like it was going to jump out of my body. Every inch of my skin warmed.

Akacia turned so that we were face to face and her hand came up to cup my cheek. I rested my hands on her waist. Her gaze darted from my eyes to my lips. She muttered something about hesitation and then her soft, supple lips were on mine. It was my turn to be surprised. Nobody had ever been so bold, but I was only startled for a beat before I seized her lips and deepened the kiss.

When Akacia pulled away the tiniest of moans escaped my mouth. A smile played on her lips that I swear tasted like honey. She tangled her hands in my hair at the back of my neck.

There was a knock on the door. "Do you need help?"

Akacia giggled and I answered, "No. Just another minute."

God, I loved the sound of her laugh.

"I should get dressed."

I nodded and went back to my dressing room to get back in my clothes. I stood quietly for a moment just thinking about the kiss that we just shared. She was so beautiful and I felt different when I was with her. So alive. I wanted to hold her and keep her safe. I wanted to get to know who she was and make her happy. Why did it have to be her? The Empress that Caspar wanted so badly. Why did I have to fall for her?

As we walked down the corridor, I asked, "What was that thing you said back in the dressing room?"

Her eyes narrowed for a minute before they widened. "Without hesitation. It's a motto. To live life without hesitation."

It was late into the night and I thought about staying in a room at the space station. My thoughts drifted to asking Kaci to stay with me, even if we did nothing but lay in bed together. Just being next to her made me feel a sort of contentment that I had never experienced before. Maybe I could take her to have her feet massaged and then I'd ask her if she'd like to stay in a room with me.

I ran the conversation over and over in my head. Distracted and still trying to come up with the most nonchalant tone I could muster to ask her this, I glanced up ahead and my eyes landed on Lorcan, one of Caspar's men. Fear ripped through me.

"What?" Kaci asked when I came to an abrupt stop.

"You have to hide!" I said. I pushed her around the corner. Hoping that Lorcan hadn't seen us yet. "Stay there."

I stepped back out into the corridor and Lorcan's eyes locked on me.

"Everleigh, I'm surprised to see you here." Lorcan stood in front of me dressed in jeans and a black T-shirt. His gray-green eyes scrutinized me, causing an uneasiness to rise. "He's getting impatient. Do you know what happens when he gets impatient?" He backed me up against the wall. "People die."

I gripped my knife. "You better back up or you'll find out what happens when I get mad."

He pulled out his gun and pressed it into my side. "Keep the knife where it is. I'd kill you before you got it out anyway."

"I'm pretty sure I could throw this dagger in your eye before you kill her. Is that a chance you want to take?" Kaci stepped out, holding the dagger in her hand.

Shit!

Lorcan's eyes widened. He looked both surprised and pissed. He took a step backward and put the gun back in his holster. "No problem, pretty lady, I'm leaving. You know what Caspar wants. Deliver it before it's too late." He stalked off.

"What was that about?"

"You should have stayed hidden." I growled.

"A simple thanks for saving your life would have been fine."

"You don't understand!" I yelled. "We need to get back on the Nirvana." I paged everyone else back to the ship.

"What is it?" Zabe asked with a frown on his face when he reached the maintenance bay.

"Caspar's people are here. One saw us." I was so angry. Angry at myself for letting my guard down. Angry at Kaci for not staying hidden.

"Get her on the ship," I ordered and turned to Jago. "Is she ready?"

"Almost. I need about twenty minutes."

I pushed money into his hand. "Do it in ten."

"You got it."

I ran onto the ship and up to the bridge. Ignoring Akacia's confused look and the stares of my crew, I got the ship ready. As soon as Jago's call came that we were good to go, we took off and using the FTL drive, got far away from the space station.

"What is going on?" Akacia demanded.

Chewing on my lip, I tried to figure out what to say. "Caspar—the guy who wants us to deliver you to him—is that guy's boss."

Her face turned ashen. "Oh."

"We'll keep you safe," I said. "It's late. We should get some sleep. I'll walk you to your room."

I felt everyone's eyes follow us as I ushered Kaci off the bridge.

Standing outside her room, she turned to me. "Thanks for today."

I gave a nod.

I could tell she was waiting, maybe hoping for another kiss. When I didn't come closer, she averted her eyes, and bit down on her lip.

"Goodnight," I said softly.

As I turned and walked away, I felt lower than I ever have. I wanted to run back to her, take her in my arms, and bury my face in her hair, but I couldn't do that. I had to figure out a way to either make all of us disappear or get her home.

<hr>

The call came after I left Akacia in her room. I stood over the controls, my hand frozen in the air, not wanting to answer it.

"Ever…" Zabe said from behind.

I growled and then hit the button. Caspar's ugly mug popped up on the screen. My stomach churned and I swallowed to keep the bile down.

"I was beginning to think you were going to double-cross me."

Play it cool. Don't give any indication you're having second thoughts. "No, sir. We've had ship problems."

"Do you not think I know your FTL drive was fixed today, yet you are not on your way here?"

My heart came to a halting stop. How did he know that?

"Lorcan contacted me, said your ship was at the space station, and there was a woman who looked like she should be wearing a crown with you."

My heart fell through the floor. He had definitely recognized her.

"What are you going to do with her?" I asked.

"I just need information."

"So you're not going to kill her?"

"No. I need her alive. And come on, Everleigh, you know better. *I* don't kill people. However, you do seem to need a reminder that the fate of your people rests in my hands." He turned then and behind him was Archer, one of my cousins, gagged and tied up. One of Caspar's men stepped forward, raised his gun, and, while I watched, without so much as a flinch, put a bullet in his head. I wanted to scream, but couldn't. All I could do was watch as his body dropped to the ground. A bloody splatter marked the wall where Archer was standing just a moment ago. This sight would haunt me forever and I deserved that. Unshed tears burned my eyes and I hated Caspar even more.

"You will turn over the Empress upon your arrival tomorrow. For every hour that you're late, I will kill another one."

Clenching my fists, I gave a hard nod and ended the call.

After a long silence, Huxley said, "It's the only way, Ever. You know that."

I did know and I hated it. I hated that he had control over me. I hated that it would take too long to figure out how to kill him. I hated that I had allowed these feelings for Kaci to compromise the safety of my family. I hated that even though my cousin had been murdered right before my eyes, I was still trying to figure out a way to avoid turning her over to Caspar.

As Briar rerouted the ship, I said, "I want him dead. And Briar, find out how he knows where we're going."

Huxley followed me to my quarters.

"What do you want?" I growled once we stood outside of my door.

He looked away.

"You want to make sure I go through with it, aren't you?" I shoved him.

"They'll kill our families. You know this. She's one girl. Sacrifice her and save all the others."

I punched him and he let me.

"It's not fair."

"I know."

Huxley let me hit him over and over until the tears started flowing, and then he gathered me in his arms and held me close.

———————⚬⚬⚬———————

"Ever?" Briar's voice was somber through my earpiece.

"Yeah?"

"We're here."

I'd spent most of the night soaking my pillow with tears, dreading the thing I had to do this morning. There was no way around it. I couldn't think about what might happen to Akacia, couldn't waste time. I had to hand her over now. Huxley and I stood in front of Akacia's door and waited for her to come out.

Maybe it was the look on our faces. Maybe it was the gun in Huxley's hand. But she knew.

"What's going on?" Her blue eyes were no longer full of wonder and curiosity. Instead they were full of fear and panic. "Everleigh?"

My throat was dry and tears pricked my eyes. "It's time for you to go."

"Go where?"

I couldn't look in her eyes. She knew.

"You don't have to do this."

"It's the job. Nothing personal." I kept my face stoic, though I was crumbling inside.

"Return me home and I'll see you're well taken care of," she pleaded.

"I can't."

"I'll give you three times what they're paying you."

"It's not the money."

"You said it's the job."

"I have to do what's right for my people."

"I'll help."

"You can't! Akacia, you have to let it go." I couldn't even bring myself to call her Kaci anymore. Kaci was what friends call her. I wasn't her friend. Friends didn't hand over their friends to evil people.

"Let it go? This is my life. These people will kill me."

"No. They said they just needed to talk to you."

"You think they're telling the truth?"

I had to believe they were. If I let myself believe that they were going to kill her, I wouldn't be able to hand her over. And I had to. I had to because my people needed to be kept safe. "I'm sorry." It came out in a whisper.

"You said I'd be safe. You—" Her voice broke. She looked around the room, hoping to find an ally. Her eyes came to a stop on me again. "I hate you."

I nodded. It was what I expected, but my heart still broke into pieces.

Huxley took her weapons from her and then led her down the corridor. He had a firm grip on her, but that didn't stop her from trying to get free. She even punched him a few times, and he took it. Just like he had taken it from me.

Standing at the airlock, Huxley asked, "Do you want one of us to walk her over?"

"No. This is something I have to do."

I forced back tears as my throat burned and wished that Caspar would take me instead. I hated myself for what I was about to do.

Akacia wasn't going without a fight. I didn't blame her. She started lashing out, kicking and broke away. She took off down the corridor, but Huxley was faster. He tackled her to the ground and ordered Zabe to zip tie her wrists together. They pulled her up to her feet and turned her around. My eyes locked with hers and I saw the pure hatred she had for me. I knew I deserved it. I had promised she'd be safe and I'd get her home, but instead I betrayed her. She was right to hate me.

"I'm sorry," I said again as I gently placed a gag in her mouth.

The glare I received would forever be etched in my mind.

I led her down the corridor to where we were docked to Caspar's ship. The door opened. Caspar and one of his guards stood there. Akacia started to thrash again.

"Oh, a feisty one," the guard said, as his gaze slid up and down her body.

Bile rose in my throat. I wanted to take him out.

"It's about time, Everleigh. You're lucky. I was trying to decide who I was going to kill next." He looked at Akacia and then ordered, "Take her."

The guard grabbed Akacia's arm and led her away.

"Nobody else gets hurt," I confirmed.

Caspar sighed. "They're safe, for now. I'll contact you when I have another job for you. But, Everleigh, when I do, don't make the same mistake. If I ever find out you are double-crossing me again, I'll kill all of your people and you." He pushed a button and the door hissed closed.

In the privacy of my quarters, tears flooded my eyes and I cried until my body shook with sobs and my throat grew raw. No longer able to suppress the rage I felt at the situation, I kicked at the desk chair and it moved a few inches. Fury filled me and I grabbed the chair and threw it against the wall. I swiped everything off my desk in one fierce, sweeping motion. I tore apart my room and screamed at the top of my lungs. I didn't stop until everything was destroyed.

I was a complete and utter mess. Feeling like I couldn't breathe, I tugged at my shirt, and screamed until I got it off. It hurt. This thing I had done and couldn't undo.

I slid down the wall and sat on the floor, tears flowing freely.

I brought my knees up to my chest and hugged them.

That was how Huxley found me hours later.

CHAPTER FIVE

AKACIA

THE DOOR BEHIND ME HISSED shut and with it all hope. I thought maybe it had been a ploy. That there was a plan. Or that Everleigh wouldn't go through with it. But she had. She handed me over. Something inside me changed. My heart hardened.

Someone pushed me from behind. "Move."

Swinging my right elbow upward, I hit the guard behind me in the gut. He pushed me up against the wall and backhanded me. I kneed him in the groin. Once he doubled over, I brought my knee to his face.

"Bitch!" he yelled and threw me against the wall slamming my head against it. Black spots exploded in my vision and my stomach churned.

"Steel! I need her to answer questions. Can you keep her conscious, please?"

"Yes, sir."

Steel grabbed a handful of my hair and forced me down the corridor to a dark, bare room. Shackles lined the base of the walls and a few hung from the sides as well. The smell of copper and death filled my lungs. This room was where people died. I wouldn't come out of this room alive.

They led me to a chair and pushed me down in it. The back of my head pounded and my vision was still fuzzy, but I could make out the guns in the hands of both guards.

"Empress. How nice to finally meet you face-to-face." A man with inky, spiked hair stood in front of me. "I'm going to remove the gag. I hope you're smart enough to know that screaming won't help. You're on my ship. Nobody here will help you. It'll only give me a headache and I don't like headaches, so I might be tempted to take that out on you. Understand?"

I didn't answer.

He reached around and cut off the gag with a knife. "Do you know who I am?"

Well, yes, sort of, but I didn't answer him. I would live longer if I didn't answer his questions. Maybe I could buy enough time to formulate an escape or for Ever and her crew to rescue me. I didn't want to believe she had just turned me over to a man who would most certainly kill me. She wasn't that heartless…or was she?

"I'm Caspar. Do you know why you're here?"

I kept quiet.

"I need answers." He paced around me. "Your father was a scientist. He was experimenting with splicing DNA. Did you know that?"

My father was into cutting edge research and technology, but I knew nothing of splicing DNA. I wasn't even sure I knew what that meant.

"Twenty-one years ago, the first splicers were born. Human with strands of animal DNA to make them faster, stronger, better. They were bred to be guards and soldiers. Nine years later, your father was murdered, and all the research vanished. I've been trying to recreate what your father did for a long time. I'm tired. I just want access to his work, his experiments. Give it to me and I'll let you go."

I had no idea what he was talking about. If he knew I didn't know would he let me go or kill me? Did it matter? "I don't know anything about his research."

He was quiet for a moment as he continued to pace around me. "Maybe not. It could be that you don't know anything or it could be that you do and don't want to tell me or you might know something you don't realize you know. Maybe you know of a secret hiding place. Or someone he worked with that got away?"

"I was seven."

"Well, nevertheless, we'll try to jog your memory." He looked at the two men who stood behind him. One was the guy from the space station. The other was the guy who walked me in here. "Lorcan, let's start with you."

"Let me at her," Steel growled, nursing his injuries.

They took turns using my face and body as a punching bag. I lost count after fourteen hits. Tears pricked my eyes, but I kept them from falling.

"Stop," Caspar ordered. "Have you remembered anything yet, Empress?"

My teeth felt loose and my mouth was full of blood. I glared at Caspar and spat at him. I could feel my face swelling. There was nothing more I could say. They could do whatever they wanted to me, but I was just going to stay quiet. If I ended up dead, then so be it.

"Again," he ordered and the beating resumed. And then, once again, Caspar stopped it and asked me if I remembered anything. It was an endless cycle and I tried to go somewhere in my head where the pain didn't reach.

"Maybe some time alone will help. Let her think about things." They tossed me to the floor. Loran snapped the metal shackles into place around my ankles. Only after giving the chain a hard tug to make sure it was secure did he cut the zip tie around my wrists. Seconds later I was alone. I curled into a ball and let the sobs come. Exhausted from the beating, I fell asleep soon after.

When I woke I didn't know how long I had slept. Could have been minutes or hours. My bruised and probably broken body was stiff from sleeping on the cold floor. A loud growl cramped my stomach, so I knew it had been long enough to get hungry. It was quiet and they didn't come. Nobody came. I sat up and yanked at the chain. I kicked the wall. And when that didn't work, I sat against the wall and stared at nothing.

The quiet made me think about things that I didn't want to think about. The kiss I shared with Everleigh was among those things. It played over and over in my mind. I tried to push it down. Tried to block it out. Tried not to think about it. But the more I did, the more it surfaced, taunting me and making me feel guilty and naïve.

How warm she was. How soft she was. How perfectly our lips had fit together.

How could she betray me? Those kisses were nothing but empty promises. Nothing but lust.

I hung onto that anger when Caspar's men finally came back and took off the shackles only to hook me up to different ones. There was no give in the chains that spread me out like an X. Then, for who knows how long, I was punched, kicked, and even whipped a couple times. When none of that worked, they got out a chain and whacked me across the back with it. My mind went to that hatred and betrayal I felt for Everleigh and stayed there. I fought to stay conscious so that I could hear what they were saying.

"What if she really doesn't know?"

"Or maybe she was trained to withstand torture?"

"Let me have some fun with her, boss." I think it was Lorcan who spoke, but my head was pounding so hard, I wasn't positive.

I felt a hand on my butt, but there was nothing I could do about it.

"No. Give her some water, so she doesn't die of dehydration. Let her go hungry a little longer, then we'll up the tactics."

The next thing I knew someone was pouring water in my face. I wanted to refuse, but I was thirsty, so I gulped it down.

They left me hanging there, but that was okay. I slipped into the darkness that had been waiting for me.

CHAPTER SIX

AKACIA

A S THE VOICES NEARED, I stayed still, wanting to get a sense of what was going on.

"I'm telling you, she looks better than she did before. She was all cut up, bruised, and swollen, but her skin looks almost flawless now," a voice said.

I was rolled onto my back and someone's rough hands pushed my hair away from my face. "Could it be...no... maybe..."

Caspar was close. I could smell garlic on his breath.

My eyes popped open. I lunged forward, grabbing Caspar by the neck and squeezing. I kneed him in the gut and forced him onto his back. I pressed harder and his face turned a deep shade of red.

Someone pulled me off of him. I caught a blow to the face and tasted blood. I waited for the next blow, but instead Caspar grabbed my face. "Watch that wound. Let me know how it looks later," he wheezed. "No water or food today."

When they left, I pushed myself against the wall and closed my eyes, welcoming the darkness again.

I was being dragged somewhere. I felt weak and hungry, but not in any extreme pain. They placed me on a cold table.

This was new. Now what?

"Run the machine," Caspar ordered.

Machine? What machine? What were they doing? I didn't ask though. I wouldn't give them the satisfaction. A hum came from below and a strange blue light filled the room and they both disappeared.

"Well, I'll be damned," Caspar said from somewhere to the far right.

My eyes darted to him wondering what he had just found.

"There was a rumor that your father had finally perfected nanites to be used for healing," he said, almost in awe, as he examined my skin. "It was said that someone close to him had been mortally injured and he had fixed them. It must have been you. You were hurt, almost dead, and your father must have injected you with the nanites. They heal you. Not immediately, but quickly."

I had no idea what he was talking about, but my head was swirling with questions.

"I'm going to take a sample of your blood." He pulled out a syringe and jabbed it into my arm and filled the vial.

"Lorcan, we need to change our methods." Caspar looked back down at me. "Unless of course, you're ready to talk."

I turned away from him. I knew nothing, but he'd never believe me.

"Take her."

This time I was put in some sort of choke collar, forcing me to stand. I was weak. Beyond exhausted. I no longer cared about anything. I was given only a few sips of water. Hunger pains gripped my stomach. Every time I fell asleep, my body would go slack, causing the collar to choke me, forcing me awake and to my feet once again.

I still had no answers for them when they came to question me.

"She's still weak and tired, so the nanites do nothing for her there," Caspar said to himself more than anybody else, like he was experimenting on me. "You can still die, you know."

My mind wasn't clear enough to think about what he was saying. I didn't care. I wished they'd just kill me and get it over with.

They released the collar and I fell to the floor, too weak to stand. Lorcan grabbed a fistful of my hair, dragged me across the room, and shoved my face into a basin of water and held me under. My lungs burned. After a few seconds, he yanked my head out. I gasped for breath.

"Answers? No?"

My head was submerged again. I thrashed, trying to break free. He held me under a bit longer this time, until I started to kick and grab at his hands.

"Anything?" he asked, once he'd yanked me out.

I fought against him, but he easily overpowered me and plunged my face into the water again. Water forced its way past lips that I desperately tried to keep shut. It burned as it trickled down my trachea. The fingers in my drenched hair tightened and yanked my head out of the water. I tried to breathe, but all I could do was cough.

The next dunk was longer and my lungs screamed for air. *Be strong. Stay strong. Don't let them break you.* I focused on the betrayal. My hatred. That was what kept me from just giving in.

Two more times he dunked me, and just when I felt myself slipping, Caspar yelled for them to quit.

"Let her think about this. Tomorrow, we'll start cutting off fingers or toes, maybe taking some teeth. I suggest, Empress, you think about if protecting this information is worth losing your body parts."

Lorcan dragged me over to the wall and locked the chain around my ankle. Wet and exhausted, I succumbed to the darkness quickly.

CHAPTER SEVEN

EVERLEIGH

I SAT UP IN BED GASPING for breath. The nightmare had woken me up again. Akacia was falling and I couldn't catch her. I couldn't save her.

"Just a dream," I said out loud to myself over and over again. But it wasn't. It wasn't just a dream. She was out there, with that creep, and I was responsible for that.

At first, I tried not to let this torment me. I was the commander of the ship. I had made the best decision under those circumstances and I needed to move on. But the weight of the decision crushed me.

I had to fix this and the only way I could fix it was to kill Caspar.

My every waking moment was spent thinking up a plan to kill him. It wasn't going to be easy and I might die doing it, but I had to try. It was the only way to rescue Akacia and keep my people safe. I knew she hated me. I doubted she'd ever forgive me. But I couldn't live with myself if I didn't try.

"This won't work, Ever," Huxley said when I pitched a plan. "It won't work. I know you're hurting, but we can't go in there with a half-assed plan like this. We'll all get killed."

"Screw you."

Huxley sighed. "Ever—"

"What if you could rescue her? Kill him later, but rescue her now?" Briar interrupted.

I looked up at her. "What?"

"What if we were to take the Artemis, cloaked of course, get close enough to Caspar's ship and jump. We could grab her and jump back out of there."

I stared at her for a minute and then walked to the window. "His ship is ten times the size of ours. How will we know where to jump to?"

"I'm pretty sure I know where they would keep her. Well, I've narrowed it down to two places," Briar said.

"How do we know he still has her or hasn't killed her?" Zabe asked and I shot him a look.

"She is alive," Briar blurted.

"How do you know?" I demanded.

She hesitated.

"What?"

"I didn't know if I should show you—"

"Briar, just tell me!"

"I've been monitoring a few different things. Tapped into some conversations. Hacked a few databases. I discovered a transmission that was sent to Valinor demanding research materials or Caspar would kill her."

"And?"

She sighed. "Zia, play video."

Caspar appeared onscreen. "I have your Empress. She's alive for now, but she won't be for long, unless you send over all of her father's research."

The man Akacia had called Galton responded, "We want proof of life."

"Of course."

My hand flew up to my face as the camera flipped to show Akacia curled up in a ball on the floor, bloody and beaten, but alive.

"From this video, I was able to narrow the room down," Briar said.

"You've been looking for a way to help her all this time?" I asked.

Briar bit on her bottom lip and shrugged. "I like her."

"You never cease to amaze me. Thank you."

"We all liked her, Ever. We just love our families," Huxley muttered.

"I know! Don't you think I know? You guys are my closest friends. You are my family. I don't want to let you down. I don't want to hurt you. But...this girl...she's..." I searched for the right words but couldn't find them. Thankfully they understood.

"We know," Briar said. "And that's why I kept looking."

Huxley sighed. "You can't go alone."

"Bri needs to stay with the ship," Zabe said.

"I'll go," Huxley said. "You and me. We'll go get her."

I smiled at him. "How long until we can get close enough?"

"We can be there in twelve earthhours. It won't take long for you to get the Artemis close enough. Caspar has an alarm system on his ship, but I can hack in and let you know when you can jump."

"Where do we go?" It had been a long time since I had been on Caspar's ship. When he took us from our parents, we lived on his ship for years while he trained us. Just thinking about being there made me sick. I had blocked out so much of what happened there and I worried going back would trigger those memories.

Briar pulled up a map of Caspar's ship on the big screen and highlighted the two rooms she thought Akacia could be in. They weren't close to each other, but they weren't clear across the ship either. I could do this. I could get in and get out, but I had to go alone. I couldn't risk anyone else's lives.

"If we do this, he will kill our families."

We all stood in silence thinking about that until Huxley said, "Do you really think we'll ever find them?"

Briar held up a tiny little metal object. "It's a tracker. There's a reason I chose that closet. When you jump into that closet, Ever, stick this there. I can control it from here. Not only will I be able to track his ship, but I should be able to hack into their comms and see who they're talking to."

"You're a genius." Looking at them all, I said, "This is something we all need to be in agreement on. There's a good chance she'll hate us and our families will be killed. Most likely, he'll come after us."

Briar, Huxley, and Zabe nodded. "Go get her."

Smiling, I turned to leave and get ready, but Briar stopped me. "Ever!"

"Yeah?"

"I found the tracker on our ship."

Spinning back around, I growled. "Tell me."

"I took care of it. I hacked in and sent it a virus. Next time we're at a station, we can have it removed. It's a lot bigger than the one I just gave you and it's on the outside of the ship."

"I want to know how it got there in the first place!" It infuriated me that there was either a traitor at one of the space stations or the tracker had always been there.

"I'll find out," Briar answered.

I went to the weapons training room and after pounding out my anger on the punching bag. I spent some time training with different weapons. After that I ate a good meal. I had to keep up my strength. With nothing else to do, I stood at the window on the bridge for a while and thought about Akacia. It had been ten nights since I handed her over—ten nights since I've slept.

As I walked by the room she had slept in on my way to the med bay, I turned and walked in. Something by the bed caught my eye. I crossed the room and picked up the ring. Kaci's ring. I ran my finger over her family crest and felt a tear slip down my cheek. I needed to get this back to her. I placed it in a drawer in my room for safekeeping.

In the med bay, I found an adrenaline patch. I placed it on my stomach and waited for the burst of energy to hit me. With the adrenalin pumping through my veins, I hurried to the weapons room where I chose a knife and a gun. I walked briskly to the bridge and examined the map one more time.

I heard Briar approaching from behind. "You're going alone, aren't you?"

"It's too dangerous," I responded, grabbing one of the jump devices.

She nodded and handed me the tracker. "Be careful and bring her back."

I placed my hand on her arm. "Thank you."

The Artemis was easy for one person to man. I powered it up and blasted off.

"Everleigh! What are you doing?" Huxley's pissed off voice came through my earpiece the moment I'd drifted free of the Nirvana.

"Sorry, Hux. I have to do this myself."

"You're going to get yourself killed!"

"I've got this, Hux. Just be ready. She'll need medical help."

Time seemed to stretch on forever. My leg bounced up and down and my fingers wouldn't stop tapping the control board. Would she be okay? She had to be okay. What if I was too late? What if I found her dead? What then? I wasn't sure I would be able to jump back off that ship. I would kill him right then and there. Or be killed.

With the Artemis the perfect distance away from Caspar's ship, I double checked my weapons, and took out the jump device. "On your word, Briar."

A few seconds later, she said, "Go now. I will keep it down as long as I can."

"Okay. I'm going in."

"Good luck, Ever," Huxley said with a sigh.

I entered the location of a small closet near the first room. Taking a deep breath and closing my eyes, I pushed the button. When my eyes opened, I was in the closet on Caspar's ship. The space was cramped but the door was already open. I dug out the tracker from my pocket and stuck it in the corner on the floor. I peeked out into the corridor. The coast was clear. Quickly and quietly, I darted over to the room and peered inside. Empty.

The second room was down the hall. Getting there didn't take long, yet it felt like it took forever. Double-checking the corridor for guards, I slipped around the corner and down to the room.

My heart stopped when I looked into the room. Bile rose in my throat and I forced it back down. Akacia was there, on the ground, chained like an animal, dripping wet. She looked up at me with feral eyes.

This was my fault.

Fury took over and I gripped my gun looking for someone to blame and kill for treating her like this. Nobody was in the room but her. Assessing the situation, I had to get her out of the chains and then I could jump with her.

Someone was whistling from the corridor behind me. I slipped inside the room and waited. In a singsong voice, a man called, "Time to lose some fingers."

As soon as he stepped across the threshold, I threw a high kick, knocking him back. He slammed me against the wall. I threw a looping punch that hit him in the head and he staggered back enough for me kick him in the chest. I slammed his head into the wall. He kicked me and I flew, landing on my back. I wrapped my legs around his and tripped him up, sending him crashing to the ground next to me. I reached for the knife at my hip and stabbed him in the neck, killing him.

I used his shirt to wipe the knife clean, and put it back in my scabbard. I searched his pockets for keys and sighed with relief when I found them. Tears stung my eyes as I scrambled over to Akacia. I blinked them back. This was not the time or the place to get emotional. Still in my clothes, she tried to drag herself away, but she was too weak to get more than an inch. With the cuffs unlocked, I carefully picked her up in my arms and hit the jump button.

I set her down gently and speaking into the earpiece, I said, "I've got her. We're on our way back."

"Copy that, Commander," Briar answered.

We were back on the Artemis. It almost seemed too easy.

But before I could even complete that thought, the ship lurched and alarms started going off.

"Damn!" I punched buttons and took the wheel. It rocked

again. "They're firing at us. Somehow they found us and they're attacking."

Silence.

"Nirvana? Can you hear me? Nirvana, this is your commander. Come in."

Nothing.

Aiming our weapons at Caspar's ship, I fired, hitting, but not causing much damage. They fired back and the Artemis started spinning. Studying the GPS, I noticed a small planet not too far away. I grabbed the manual controls and steered toward it.

The planet got bigger and bigger and we rushed toward it far too quickly. Reality hit me as we entered the planet's gravitational pull. We were going to crash. I couldn't land, but I slowed the speed of the ship and brought up our shields hoping they'd protect us a little from the heat of entry, maybe even the crash.

We came in fast and I braced myself against the controls. As we slammed into the ground, my head hit the control panel and blackness surrounded me.

I startled awake with a gasp. My head pounded and there was some blood on the panel in front of me. I touched the place where the pain originated and winced. It wasn't gushing, so it was just a minor cut. There was a burning smell that made me gag. I breathed in through my mouth so I wouldn't throw up. Where were we? Looking around it all came flooding back to me. I was in the Artemis and it had crashed. But where was…

"Akacia!" I spun around to where I had laid her down. She wasn't there.

A flash of red caught my eye. Blood. Supplies and debris covered the spacecraft. I made my way over to it and pushed away a piece of metal that had fallen on top of her. Rolling her onto her back, I assessed her injuries. She had a nasty gash on her head, much worse than the one I had on mine. Her lips were cracked. Her skin pale. And she looked twenty pounds lighter than the last time I had seen her. She was still somewhat wet and I could only imagine why.

There was another wound on her side, but the head injury concerned me the most. I ripped a piece of cloth and pressed it to her head.

I checked her pupils for responsiveness and was relieved to find that she was still alive. The bleeding was my first concern and hopefully she would wake up soon. I cradled her head in my lap and leaned back against the wall. Besides Akacia, I had two major concerns. I wasn't sure if we had landed on a friendly planet and there was Caspar. Would he follow us here to complete the job?

We couldn't stay in the ship.

I ran the back of my hand along Akacia's face and my thumb traced her lips. My lips ached to kiss hers. My arms ached to hold her.

A quick peek under the cloth and I could see that the bleeding hadn't stopped. There was a medical kit near the door. I gently rearranged Akacia and grabbed the kit. Once I had the wound clean and dressed. I rushed to the controls and pushed a few buttons, hoping they still worked.

The Artemis' onboard computer analyzed data collected from the planet's environment and I surmised that the atmosphere was safe. We could breathe. No poisons registered. Temperature was good. That was a relief. I checked the GPS to see if it could tell me what planet we were on, but it wasn't working. I tried the radio again and got nothing.

Next, I assessed the rest of the ship. There was a gaping hole in the floor, the engines wouldn't switch on, and the cloaking didn't work. There was no flying this thing out of here. There was no flying it ever again. I needed to take a look outside and see where we were.

The door was stuck. I had to slam into it a few times to before it flew open and I stumbled outside. I took a few deep breaths to test the air even though the readings said it was fine. It was thick and humid, but breathable. We had crashed into a forest of giant mushroom-like trees whose leaves were on top, facing the sun. Their wide trunks were tangled with winding vines and had no low branches. With lots of thorny plants growing underneath the tall trees, the smaller brush looked just as friendly. The trees would provide cover and shelter, but if Caspar saw us go down, he would probably be back to make sure we were dead. There was no way I could move the ship. It was too big to hide. It needed to be destroyed. There was a self-destruct button. Once I hit it, I had one minute to get us to safety. Then if Caspar did come looking, he'd only find the wreckage. Hopefully, he'd assume we were dead. Of course that meant that if my crew came looking for us, they'd assume we were dead, too. No matter what I chose, we were screwed.

Back inside, I tore apart the rest of the ship looking for food or water, knowing that there wasn't any. I found a thin blanket and some rope and grabbed them. I took inventory of the weapons and put as many on my person as I could.

Akacia moaned. I hurried back to her and cupped her face in my hands. "Akacia? Can you hear me?"

She moaned again and turned her head a bit.

"Akacia? Open your eyes."

She blinked a couple times and I knew when she could focus because her eyes showed every emotion she was experiencing— relief, happiness, hurt, pain, fear. I hated that I had that effect on her. "Are you okay?"

Her blue eyes, dark with betrayal, narrowed and she looked away.

"You have a head wound. It's bleeding. We need to get out of here. Caspar will come after us." I kept my sentences short and emotionless. "Do you think you can walk?"

She made no effort to answer, but swallowed and tried to get up. As soon as she was on her feet, she lost her balance and started to fall. I reached out and caught her. "Okay, Empress, I'll carry you."

She was heavy, but I was strong. I scooped her up. Her eyes fluttered closed again. Taking a deep breath, I hit the self-destruct button and hightailed it out of there. I ran as fast as I could with her thrown over my shoulder and found a spot behind a nearby tree. The boom rocked the ground under my feet and the heat from the explosion reached us where we huddled together, but thankfully we were unharmed by flying debris or fire. Within minutes, the ship was destroyed. I hoped I did the right thing.

Akacia didn't wake up as I walked. At least an hour had passed when I spotted a cave. I set her down outside while I went in to see if it was safe. It was small, but dry. I set her inside and then stretched. It was warm, but I didn't know how chilly it would get in the evening. I should get a fire going just in case and by the look of her lips, Akacia needed water.

I checked under the bandage first. The bleeding had stopped. I closed my eyes for a second, thanking whoever was listening for that small favor. I hated leaving her, but I had to. I found the firewood pretty quickly, but water was another story.

As I built the fire at the mouth of the cave, ominous black clouds rolled in faster than I had ever seen and a brilliant shock of white ripped through the gray sky. Another lightning bolt hit a nearby tree, cracking it in half. Way too close for comfort. The smell of the burnt tree tickled my nose.

"Shit," I swore. The fury of the storm was incredible, but where was the water? If it would rain, we'd have something to drink. Not that I had anything to collect it in. That should be my next priority. Finding something to hold water.

Lightning crashed down again and again making me very glad we were in the cave. No rain ever came. Then as quickly as the storm had appeared, it was gone.

Akacia moaned again. I looked over to make sure she was okay. Her chest rose and fell with each breath she took so at least she was still breathing.

Once the fire was roaring, I relaxed a little. My whole body ached. The bump had grown, but it wasn't bleeding anymore and the headache was manageable. I watched Akacia sleep. Peacefully sometimes, fitfully others. She grimaced. She cried out. But at least she was alive.

CHAPTER EIGHT

AKACIA

MY HEAD FELT BETTER, BUT my side was still bothering me. I knew I should rest, but I couldn't be near Everleigh. She betrayed me. She turned me over to that monster. I had to get away. I needed time. Time to think. Time to process. Time to figure out where to go from here.

I could survive on my own.

Once outside the cave, I struggled to get my feet under me. My legs were shaky, but they'd hold. I grabbed one of her knives and placed it in the scabbard on my leg.

"Where are you going?" Everleigh stood in my way. I tried to push by her, but she moved again. "You're hurt, you're dehydrated, and hungry. We don't even know where we are, if this planet has intelligent life on it, or what the terrain is."

I glared at her for a long time, and this time when I went to go by her, she let me go.

Everleigh was right though. I was hungry and weak, and I needed to find water. As I picked my way through the brush I remembered what my teachers had taught us about how to find water. Stop and listen, look for animals, and lush, green vegetation—even an increase in insects would be a good sign. Head downhill and if all else fails, find mud and dig. Once I got far enough into the trees, I sat on a rock and listened. Minutes passed and I didn't hear a damn thing that sounded like water, but maybe it was just because the pounding in my head was so loud. I looked around on the ground for animal tracks. What kind of animals lived here? Maybe there weren't any.

My wandering led me to a downward slope, it was slight, but it enough of a decline to create a puddle or a small pond from a good downpour. I quickly lost my footing on my dissent and fell to the ground. When I tried to get up the whole world spun, so I sat with my back against a tree, trying to steady myself. I was alone with my thoughts. Completely alone. Rage bubbled up and trickled over before I could stop it. I was lost on a planet I knew nothing about. There was no food or water, and very likely no way home. I drew deep breaths trying to keep from breaking down, but my body racked with sobs.

Pushing myself up, I continued on. The day wore on and I didn't find water. If I didn't find some by tomorrow, I'd be dead. Or very close to it.

I came to a clearing that led to a cliff. Inching closer, I looked over. There was a beautiful meadow below with green grass and flowers. I had to get down there. There had to be some water down there.

It would be dark soon. I should set up camp and make my way down in the morning. *Set up camp.* I laughed. It's not like I had a tent, bedroll, food, or anything like that.

I collected some twigs, but exhaustion hit before I could get a fire going. I lay down, closed my eyes and immediately drifted off to sleep.

When I woke in the morning, my body ached. My throat was parched. I licked my cracked lips and forced my eyes open. My stomach growled loudly and I thought about going back to sleep. No. I couldn't do that. I had to get up, find water and food, and figure out what to do. That was what I had to do. Right? I couldn't just let myself die here. I was the Empress of Valinor. My planet, my people needed me. My side still throbbed with pain. I pulled up my shirt and examined the wound. It was bleeding at such a slow rate, I knew I wouldn't bleed to death, but it wasn't healing.

I needed to clean it and that required water. I pushed up to my feet and began walking, stumbling every few feet, trying to find a way down.

I was getting sleepy again. Needing something to focus on to keep me alert, I thought about Everleigh. First, I thought about the kiss we shared at the space station. The one I thought would have led to more. The way her lips felt against mine. Her sweet, yet earthy scent. Feeling her heart race against my own. Then I thought about when she turned me over. Handed me to a monster like I was some kind of pawn. Something she could sell. How could she be so cruel?

My head swam. I stopped walking and I clenched my teeth, trying to steady myself. But with my eyes closed I saw Caspar coming toward me with a rope. He was going to tie me up again. Blindly, I turned and hurried through the trees, trying to find a place to hide. He was right on my heels. His laughter filled my head, sinister and taunting. I tripped and fell.

Get up! Get up and run!

My body screamed in protest, but I kept going. Was he still back there? I turned and looked back. I didn't see anything. I stopped for a moment and listened. I heard no sounds of pursuit and suddenly I realized that he might have never been chasing me at all. Starvation, dehydration, plus numerous injuries from being tortured for I didn't know how many days...all of that could cause hallucinations.

"Kace!" It was Bristow's voice.

I spun around, looking for him, before I could catch myself. "No," I said, shaking my head. I had to keep moving. These hallucinations were working against me and running blindly on a foreign planet would get me killed.

"Akacia! Wait!"

It sounded so real. Against my better judgment, I turned to look in the direction the voice came from. Bristow appeared a few feet away from me, his face frantic, sweat molding his brown hair to his brow.

"Are you real?" I asked, my voice sounded ragged and small. "Are you really here?"

"It's me, Kaci. I'm really here."

I ran toward him. "You found me!" But instead of feeling his arms wrap around me, I ran right through him.

He disappeared.

I was definitely hallucinating, but that didn't make this loss feel any less real. I dropped to my knees and wailed, not caring if anyone or anything heard me. There was something wrong with me. The skin around the wound was red and angry. Infected. If Caspar was right and I had these nanites that healed me, why wasn't I healing? Maybe he was just full of it.

Water. I needed to get to water. Just had to find my way to it.

I took a few steps, then a few more, and then fell to the ground. It was no use. I wouldn't make it. My eyes closed and I dropped weightless into the darkness.

Wet, cool, liquid, poured over my lips. I opened my mouth

and the most refreshing water I'd ever tasted soothed my dry mouth. I swallowed, coughed, and then opened my mouth for more.

My eyelids felt leaden, but I managed to open them and there was Everleigh. This must be another hallucination and I was okay with that. I didn't mind dying if she was with me. She could hold me until death came and took me away. I'd go happily. Peacefully.

"I'm here," she said. "I know you don't want me to be, but I am. I found some water not too far from here. Got a fire ready to go, too. I'm going to get you there." She put her arms under me and picked me up.

Perfect. In her arms. I rested my head on her chest and listened to her heartbeat as she carried me away. Dying in her arms seemed like a good ending. I let my eyes close again.

<hr/>

"Wake up!"

It took a minute, but I finally managed to open my eyes. Death was supposed to be quieter than this.

"I need you to understand what's going on. Your head looks fine, which is just weird, but there's another wound on your side. There's something in it. I can get it out, but you have to let me."

Maybe it wasn't a hallucination?

More water dribbled in my mouth. I could barely make out the cloth she was squeezing above my lips.

"I will wash it best I can, but there's no way to close it up. No tape. Nothing."

My focus sharpened for a moment and I thought back on survival class. I pointed to the fire and then to her knife. She looked back and forth and her eyes went wide, but she took the knife and put it on a rock over the fire. She left and returned with a stick. "Only thing I could find." She held it out to my mouth and I let her put it in and I bit down.

Everleigh wiped the wound with a cloth, and then squeezed water onto it. She took a deep breath and stuck her fingers in the wound on my side.

The pain…a pain like I'd never experienced before ripped through me. The muffled scream I let out seemed only to touch the very edges of how much it hurt. My fingers grasped at the ground beneath me. I felt her fingers as they fished around for whatever was in there. Finally she pulled it out and looked at it. "Metal."

Using the cloth, she washed the wound again. She took the knife, almost glowing red, and our eyes met. I nodded. She took the knife and pressed it to the wound in quick bursts. I chomped down on the stick, screaming. Death was definitely not this agonizing, this was living.

Once my heart stopped racing and my breathing returned to normal, I licked my lips.

"Here. Eat." She pressed something to my lips.

I squinted, trying to see what it was.

"They're berries of some sort. Not immediately poisonous or I'd be dead. Figured it's better than nothing."

I opened my mouth and let her pop a few of them in. Bursts of sweet juice filled my mouth as I chewed.

The light from the closest sunstar was already dimming. Night was falling again. My eyelids felt heavy.

"Sleep, Empress."

I kept quiet and after a minute of staring at her, wondering if this was indeed real, I closed my eyes. Guess we'd know in the next day if Caspar was right. If this wound healed, I had nanites in me.

Before my eyes even opened, I could feel a difference. No more pain. Not even soreness. Everleigh was sitting next to the fire. Her dark hair had been pulled back into braids.

She turned and our eyes met.

My heart leaped at the sight of her, the way it always had, the way it always would, but then rage broke through, boiling through my veins. A broken, guttural sob ripped up from my throat before I could stop it. I cursed myself for letting her get to me. I cursed myself for wanting to let the rage go and take her in my arms. I cursed myself for trusting her in the first place.

She got up and started coming toward me. I turned away. She didn't deserve my tears. Didn't deserve to see me like this. I wanted to be strong. Crying just showed weakness.

"Let me check your wound."

I tried to pull away from her, but my body was still weak from the lack of food and water, and she easily jerked me back. Her fingers brushed over my skin and my heart betrayed me by skipping a beat.

"You're healed." Her face twisted with confusion. "Completely." She looked from that wound up to my head where the injury had been. Then meeting my eyes, she questioned, "What are you?"

I yanked my shirt back down and pulled away. She hadn't stopped staring at me and it was becoming uncomfortable, but I had no desire to explain right now. I didn't even know if what

Caspar said was true. Though everything pointed to exactly that.

Nanites. I knew nothing about them and apparently nothing about my father. Or what had happened to me when I was younger. Curiosity alone would make me find a way to get home so I could get some answers.

Everleigh blew out a long breath. "Fine. We need to get water. There's a small stream not too far from here, but it's downhill. Seeing as you're all healed, you shouldn't have any problems."

I pushed myself to my feet and waited for her to lead.

"You can't just not talk to me."

The hell I couldn't. I had no intentions of ever speaking to her again.

Everleigh began walking. Soon we were on a downhill slope, so we angled ourselves sideways and continued down. I could hear the stream before I saw it and my tongue slid across my lips in anticipation.

Once the stream came into view, I rushed over to it, cupped my hands and drank the water. Once my thirst was quenched, I stood and looked at our surroundings. There were mountains in the distance. To my right, there were some brightly colored trees that looked similar to something on my planet. If they were, they might have fruit. I started toward them.

Everleigh put her hand on my shoulder. "Where are you going?"

I hated the way my body betrayed me. I hated that I nearly leaned into her touch before I jerked my shoulder away instead. Without saying a word, I continued to the trees. My stomach let out a loud gurgle as I got closer and saw they were indeed fruit. First I looked at the few lying on the ground. There were bite marks in them. My eyes searched the area for dead animals and I saw none. Most likely the fruit wasn't poisonous.

A few of the soft, fuzzy fruits hung on a low branch just over my head. I stretched up and grabbed one then bit into it and the juicy flesh warmed in my mouth. It was close to what grew on Valinor, but it wasn't exactly the same. Not being positive they were safe, I waited a minute to make sure I didn't drop dead. When I didn't, I quickly finished the rest of it and grabbed another one off the tree. Everleigh had caught up to me and was chowing down on one.

Neither of us said a word. We sat in silence. The air was so thick with tension that it seemed to hum around us. Everleigh started collecting firewood again and built a fire.

At the stream, I rinsed off some of the dirt and blood from my hands before drinking more water. I felt as if I couldn't get enough to drink. I was forever thirsty and hungry. It would be dark soon. The walk back to the fire seemed so far, and I thought about just sleeping where I was. Away from her.

I should leave. Go off on my own again. But I was weaker than normal and not sure I'd get too far.

Plus part of me knew I couldn't leave her. And that pissed me off. She handed me over to a madman, but walking away from her broke me.

Back at the fire, I laid down with my head on my arm. She took one last look at me and then did the same across from me. Wordlessly, we stared at each other. How could she betray me? Hadn't that kiss meant anything to her? Before she could see the tears in my eyes, I closed them and let sleep come.

Caspar grabbed me and held my head under the water. I thrashed trying to get free. My lungs were burning. I couldn't breathe.

I sat straight up, gasping for breath.

"You're safe," Everleigh said from her crouched position in front of me. "You're having a nightmare."

Turning to her, I could see the water in her eyes, shimmering in the moonlight, and my stupid heart clenched, thankful that she was here with me. The fear I felt in my dream didn't leave me though. My chest tightened and I felt like I couldn't catch my breath. I was warm and my head felt all fuzzy as the fear tightened its hold on me. He'd find me. He'd capture me again. I'd never be safe. My heart took off at a gallop and I yanked on my shirt.

I didn't realize she wasn't in front of me anymore until I felt her behind me. She scooted up right against my body and put her arm around me. "I've got you. You're safe."

I hated that her arms made me feel safe. I hated that my heart slowed the longer she held me. I hated that my eyes closed and I fell back to sleep in her arms.

CHAPTER NINE

EVERLEIGH

A KACIA WAS SHAKING AND CRYING. Even after seeing her beaten on that video and how she was when I found her, I hadn't thought of the after effects. Seeing her like this...I drew a shuddering breath, trying to be strong, and failing horribly.

I had to do something and there was only one thing I could think to do—hold her. I lay next to her and pulled her close. I thought she might push me away, maybe scream at me, maybe get up and move, but she didn't. After a few minutes, she actually calmed down and drifted back to sleep.

I watched her sleep for a few minutes. Her hair, tangled and a little dirty hung in her face. I gently brushed it behind her ear, repeating the motion until I fell asleep, too.

In the morning, I woke with my arm still over her. I could tell by her breathing she wasn't awake yet. My throat was dry. I should go get some water, maybe bring back some more of that fruit, but I didn't want to leave her.

After a few more minutes, I sighed and got up as quietly and carefully as I could. I wandered around the woods for a bit and collected some herbs I knew would freshen our breath.

Upon finding a fallen tree nearby, I started cutting at it. Soon I had created a small bowl. It would work. First I went back to the fruit tree and gathered a few, then I went to the stream and filled the bowl. I drank three bowls, then filled it to take back to her.

Akacia was awake when I got back to camp. Her eyes drilled into me, icy blue, and alight with fury as I knelt in front of her. She was so angry that I could feel it wafting off of her. I wasn't sure, however, if she was angry because of my betrayal or because she betrayed her own feelings when she let me comfort her.

I handed her the bowl and was happy when she took it and drank the water. I put the fruit in front of us and let her have her choice first. She chose one and ate it. Laying out the herbs, I said, "It freshens your breath."

With arched eyebrows, she took one and popped it in her mouth. I stuck the rest in my pocket.

We weren't going to find a way off the planet by just sitting here. When she was feeling better, we could venture off to find help—if there was help, but we needed to stay a few nights for Akacia to rest. Her body might be healed on the outside, but she was raw on the inside. My mind wandered a lot in the silence. I wondered how she healed. She wasn't an AI. She bled. Were all of her people like that? Was she special? I thought about if it really mattered. Did it change the way I felt about her?

Not one bit.

Days and nights continued. Some nights Akacia cried and I held her. Some nights she was calm. Some nights she didn't sleep at all.

She still didn't talk. She was healing. I gave her the time.

I said things here or there, but mostly just kept to myself and watched her.

Just before sunset, Akacia was staring at the stream, watching the water. I could tell by the way her body shook, even from behind, that she was crying. I sat next to her and put my arm around her shoulders, hoping to comfort her.

She shoved me away. Her eyes were full of fear. I held my hands up apologetically. She shook her head and jumped up. I followed. She was breaking down. Losing it. It had finally gotten to be too much. She took a swing, hitting me under my eye. I could have stopped it, but I didn't. I deserved it. She cried out and swung at me again. Her fist connected with my lip.

She waited. Waited for me to fight back.

I shook my head. My own hot tears slid down my cheeks. I wouldn't fight her.

She threw herself at me, pounding my chest with her fists. She cried out and started to collapse.

I grabbed her shoulders, steadying her, and easing her to the ground.

"I've got you."

She let me hold her while she cried. I ran my fingers through her hair and hummed. How I wished I could go back and change things. When she fell asleep, I carried her back to camp and lay next to her. I cherished every second because I never knew from one moment to the next if she was going to let me near her again. During the night, she let me hold her. In the daytime, the anger returned. Touching was off limits. I started to stand and go to other side of the fire where I could sleep, she roused and her hand searched for mine. I took it and she interlaced her fingers with mine. It was a simple gesture, one that made me warm and hopeful.

CHAPTER TEN

AKACIA

WHEN I WOKE, I COULD feel Everleigh's arm draped around me. I wanted nothing more than to turn in her arms and put my lips on hers. I dreamt of loving her, being with her, being hers. I could feel the way she felt about me when she held me. I could see it in her eyes. I began to wonder if it was possible.

I took the extra minute this morning to stay in her arms.

A rumble in the distance caused Ever to stir. She sat right up when the second rumble came. "Storm," she mumbled. "We need to take cover."

We hurried into the woods and pressed up against the trees. The lightning storm arrived with ferocity making me wish we were still at the cave. Lightning struck the ground all around us. Then came the hail. Large pieces of ice slammed into the ground. We ducked down and covered our heads. I grimaced when a piece of hail made it through the canopy of trees and hit my back. It literally felt like forever that we were stuck there, but finally the hail and lightning stopped.

"You okay?" Everleigh asked as we stood.

I ignored her and walked back to where we slept.

She continued talking, "I'm fine. Thanks. Couple of hits on my shoulders, but I'll live."

After eating, Everleigh turned to me and we stared at each other for a long time. Finally, she let out a sigh and said, "I don't know what's out there, but we need to go."

Other than putting a bunch of fruit in the blanket, we didn't have anything to pack, so we just started walking next to the stream. I stayed behind her. The temperature went up as the day wore on and I was sure I smelled ripe. I needed to wash. Maybe tonight.

We stopped before the sunstar set, building a fire, and making sure we were ready for the night. The stream was too shallow to bathe in, so I only washed my face, hands and feet.

Everleigh made two spears from wood. She handed me one. "In case we run into anything."

I haven't used a spear before. I had trained with swords, daggers, and a bow and arrow, but not a spear. I would have to ask my teachers to add that if I made it home. She set traps for animals hoping to catch one. There weren't any fruit trees around and we were down to four fruits.

When I woke the next morning, Everleigh wasn't next to me. My heart sank a little, and I chastised myself for feeling that way. She betrayed me. I couldn't fall for her. Couldn't be with her. Not the way my heart wanted.

She emerged from the tree line. "Didn't catch anything," she said, disappointment in her voice.

We walked all day. I fell back and walked slower than she did, lost in my head. At some point I looked up to find Everleigh staring ahead. Catching up to her, I saw what she saw. A huge body of water. A lake? We couldn't continue straight.

"We'll stay there tonight. Change direction tomorrow."

We set up camp by the lake. After building a fire, Everleigh disappeared into the forest. When she came back, she said, "Set some traps. Maybe we'll get lucky this time." She looked at me as if she was waiting for me to respond. When I didn't, she sighed, sat down and took off her shoes.

I closed my eyes for a while, until my stomach growled. Grabbing a piece of fruit, I got comfortable near the fire where I could watch the flames dance.

Just as I sunk my teeth in for another bite fruit, Everleigh walked by me completely naked. My chewing slowed and I swallowed hard as she charged into the lake and started washing up. Her body was absolutely perfect. I thought about the time she must spend working out to have a body like that. Besides the tattoos I had already seen, she had a massive, colorful galaxy tattoo on her right hip down to her knee. It was stunning.

Everleigh didn't acknowledge that I might be watching her or show any shame in her nudity. She just washed. I looked down at my own body and remembered how dirty I was. I probably smelled, too. Without really making a decision to do it, I stood, took off my clothes, and walked toward the lake. With the sun down, the water was chilly and stopped me in my tracks. Maybe this wasn't such a good idea.

I let out a yelp as frigid water hit my body. When I looked up, my eyes locked with Everleigh's and she laughed. I froze. It was such a beautiful sound and I hadn't heard it in so long that it sounded strange. Then she tossed more water my way. I bit down on my lip and splashed her back. A few minutes later, I was neck deep in the water. I rubbed every part of my body and then went underwater to soak my hair. The moment my head was submerged images of being held under the water filled my mind and I broke the surface of the water gasping.

Everleigh was by my side in an instant.

Everything rushed at me, warping in and out of focus.

My heart pounded in my chest and it felt like someone was squeezing the life out of me. My entire body shook violently.

"You're having another panic attack. I'm going to touch you now," she announced before putting her arms around me, she held me close. The tranquility that seemed to permeate her settled around me. My heart slowed. My breathing became more even. Everleigh watched me like she was trying to gauge how much would be okay, where my breaking point would be.

"Breathe with me," she said. I matched my inhales and exhales to hers and she smiled encouragingly. My heart slowed. I was safe. Caspar wasn't torturing me anymore.

There was a silence as still as stone between us for a few long moments as we stared into each other's eyes.

I finally broke the silence. "I hate you..."

"I know."

My lip trembled, and I lifted my hand to cup her cheek. I sought her lips with mine. The warmth of them sent a jolt to my heart. Tears flowed freely and I could taste the salt as it blended with the kiss. One of her hands was in my hair while the other was on the small of my back holding me up. My left hand wrapped around her waist. We fit together seamlessly like we were made to hold each other.

Her lips worked in tandem with mine like a hypnotic sensual dance. I whimpered at the tender emotions we shared.

When we pulled apart, I let out a soft breath, feeling slightly dazed. I opened my eyes and met hers. They were full of kindness, compassion, and maybe some guilt. She traced my lips with her thumb.

I swallowed hard and took a step back.

We didn't say anything more to each other that night. We

dressed in only our underclothes. Everleigh built a fire while I washed our clothes, then laid them next to the fire to dry.

Her trap had caught a small animal. She cooked it over the fire and we both ripped the meat off its bones.

After we ate, she sat behind me and started braiding my hair. I figured it'd get less dirty and tangled in a braid. Feeling her fingers work through my hair brought tears to my eyes again. I was glad I was facing the other way so she didn't see. When she finished, we switched places and I braided hers.

Later when I lay my head down, my heart burned with the kiss we shared earlier. I tossed and turned. My mind wouldn't stop reliving it. The feel of her lips on mine. The way her hands felt on my body. Here, in the nighttime, I wanted her to hold me forever.

Daytime brought back the anger. The feelings of abandonment crept into my thoughts. I remembered how alone I felt on Caspar's spacecraft and how alone I felt right now. I thought about the torture he put me through and how I'd never look at water the same way.

"You betrayed me! You—" my voice broke, "left me."

Everleigh's eyes went wide with pain and knowing. "I'm sorry."

"You…we…" It felt like someone was stabbing my heart with a knife. "You just handed me over like it was nothing."

"I had no choice."

"We all have choices."

"He has my family. All of our families," she explained. "If we don't do what he says, he takes it out on them."

"This is why you do things for him? To keep them safe?"

"Yes." She let out a huge sigh like she was relieved to finally tell me this. "I was trying to find a way for us to disappear and figure out how to kill him, but I didn't have time. He shot my cousin because I was late turning you over. Said he'd kill more every hour I delayed."

"You promised. You said you'd bring me home." It was childish, but I felt ripped wide open.

"I know."

"Do you know what he did to me?"

She looked away. She wasn't getting off that easy. She needed to know.

"First they beat me. Then they starved me, hung me up, and beat me some more. I was shackled to a wall, whacked with a chain, and then they tried to drown me. And what for? Information that I don't even know."

A tear escaped one of her eyes and rolled down her cheek. "I'm sorry."

"You handed me over to them." I glared at her. "I hate you."

"I know."

There was no more talking. We just walked for hours. Keeping the lake on our right, we headed away from the mountains. There was still no sign of intelligent life on this planet.

The words tumbled out of her mouth, surprising me, "It wasn't personal."

Tears stung my eyes and I sucked in a shuddering breath. "It was to me." There was a whimper in my voice I prayed she couldn't hear. I felt broken and beaten. I *was* broken and beaten.

"I didn't want to betray you. It pained me to do so, but I did what needed to be done."

"I get it. I do." I took a couple steps backward.

"You are right to be angry." She stepped closer, eliminating the space between us. "I don't know how to apologize for what I've done. I don't know how to make it right. I know I did the wrong thing and I feel horrible for it, but I don't know how to make up for it. I don't know how to apologize for the biggest mistake of my life. Saying I'm sorry doesn't seem like enough for the hurt I caused you."

Even in my anger, I found some measure of comfort in being physically close to her. "I can't just forgive you in a day. My feelings aren't like that. Healing is a process. I will say that I don't hate you as much today as I did yesterday." My throat felt tight and my eyes stung with tears I refused to let fall.

"I would sacrifice myself for you," she whispered.

"I know."

And I did know. I knew she was telling me the truth. She would have turned herself over. She would have been tortured. She would have killed herself for me. But it wasn't her life that was threatened. It had been the lives of those she loved.

I knew this, but it settled in even more and I understood. The anger had been the only thing holding me together and now it was slipping away.

"You have a knife. Do you think I should die for my betrayal?" she asked.

I sucked in a staggered breath. My heart clenched inside my chest so hard I put my hand to it. "No. No, I don't."

Another silence settled between us that went on so long my wobbling knees threatened to give out on me. My breaths came quickly as I tried to fight off the panic flowing through me.

Everleigh quickly slipped her arm around my waist, holding me up. "Breathe."

I placed my hand on her chest, hating myself for letting her hold me.

Later that night I stared into her eyes as we lay across from one another, the fire between us. "I don't know how to move on," I admitted.

"I know," she answered.

CHAPTER ELEVEN

EVERLEIGH

THE GRASS BENEATH OUR FEET was slowly fading. Up ahead was barren land. It was a dull orange color and hadn't seen water in so long that cracks ran through it in all directions. Rock formations jutted out of the ground in the distance.

We continued our trek through the desert-like area until it got dark only stopping once to shield ourselves from a dust storm. There wasn't anything to build a fire with or woods to hunt in, so we just sat staring at the stars.

I wished she would talk to me. It had been two days since her last outburst and I could tell she was still working her way through her emotions. The silence was heavy and overwhelming, but I knew that pushing her would only slow her emotional progress.

I waited until Akacia fell into a deep, restful sleep before I laid down and tried to sleep myself.

⚬⚬⚬

When we woke, there was nothing to do but continue on. Our water and food were both long gone and the desert area showed no signs of either. We needed to find the other side and fast.

It took another day until the desert started giving way to rock and before we knew it we were walking between boulders, heading downward for a while before it turned into an uphill trek. The temperature dropped the higher we climbed and I knew if I was tired, Akacia must be too. But we pushed on, hoping that we'd find refuge on the other side.

There was practically a rock wall in front of us. It wasn't too steep. I could make it, but I wasn't sure about Akacia. I glanced at her and she nodded.

We started up. She followed in my footsteps. I could have climbed faster, but purposely went slow for Akacia's sake. Each step took more and more effort, as we got higher up on the rocks. I could hear Akacia breathing heavily behind me.

We were almost there when I heard her foot slip. I spun around and grabbed her wrist before she fell. She was looking down and panting with fear. Her feet kicked wildly under her.

"Hold still!" I struggled to pull her up. Somehow I managed to get both of us over the top and fell onto my back. She landed on top of me and our eyes locked.

"Thank you…"

She rolled off me and closed her eyes, taking deep breaths. A few minutes later, she staggered to her feet and looked down.

"I wouldn't have let you fall."

She gave a slight nod.

"You're bleeding," I said. "But I suppose we don't have to worry about that."

She examined her right arm. She didn't answer and I turned around to continue on. "I didn't know," her voice seemed soft and unsure. "When I was being tortured…" It took her another minute to speak again. "Apparently I heal fast. I didn't know.

I don't remember getting hurt, so I never knew." More than anything she sounded confused and a little afraid.

"You—"

She held up her hand. "Caspar said something about my father perfecting nanites to heal injuries. I don't really know what that means. I think they're in me though."

Nanites inside of her? "They're like macro machines."

She looked over at me with tears in her blue eyes. "Does that make me a freak?"

"No." I met her eyes.

Her lip quivered.

I cupped her face and said more firmly, "No."

She nodded and licked her lips. My gaze shifted from her eyes to her mouth, but when I leaned in, she pulled back. It was daytime. We didn't do that in the daytime. That was saved for nighttime only.

We made our way over to the other side and I came to an abrupt stop.

"Shit…" I swore as I looked out over the scene in front of us. Icy spikes sprouted out of the ground. There was no flat area to walk across, no easy access to the other side.

"We have to go across that?" Akacia choked.

Ice? Snow? It couldn't be a city with a way home? Or at least a meadow with water and fruit. It had to be ice and snow? I let out a scream of frustration, kicked some rocks sent them tumbling over the side.

"Enough!" Akacia yelled, reaching out and grabbing my hand. "You won't be any good if you hurt yourself."

She was right. I knew she was right, but I was so frustrated that I couldn't stop from shaking. Why couldn't we catch a break? Were we ever going to get off this planet? Or would we be stuck here forever?

"Breathe," she said.

I sat down, put my head between my knees, and took deep breaths. After a few minutes, I looked at her. "I can't believe how lame that sounds—breathe—but I don't know what else to say."

She scoffed and her smile disappeared. "So…we have to get to the other side of the ice?"

I stood up and she followed. Behind us lay the desert, but backtracking almost seemed like a better idea than trying to get through the ice and snow in front of us. "I don't know. We don't have the clothes to keep us warm. Nothing to build a fire. We don't know how far it spans."

"You should have thought about that before rescuing me. You should have let me die there."

Spinning toward her, I said, "Our plan was a damn good one. The only way he could have known where the Artemis was is if he had the technology that can detect cloaked ships. Not many people have that."

"I don't know if I can make it. Maybe you should go. Find help."

"I'm not leaving you."

She nodded, rubbing her wrist.

"We'll stay the night here. Leave in the morning."

"Okay."

With the ice so close, as night fell, it got chillier than it had any other night. I positioned my back against a large boulder. Akacia's eyes glanced at the ground and then at me. I patted the ground in front of me. She sat in between my legs. Her back against my chest. I opened the blanket and put it over us. Then wrapped my arms around her. She nestled into me and let out a sigh.

The night was clear and we could see the stars. They were beautiful. Being on a planet made it seem surreal that I spent all my time traveling among them.

"What do you dream of?" I asked, wondering if she'd even answer.

She didn't respond right away, but then she said, "I used to dream of exploring the galaxy. Then it became to be a good leader to my people. Now, food would be great."

I laughed. "Big plates of food. Meat and vegetables."

"Dessert."

"And all the water we could drink."

"A nice soft bed," Akacia said. "And someone to fill it."

We grew quiet again and I listened to her breathing. It was rhythmic and relaxing.

Akacia ran her thumb over the tattoo on my left wrist. "Tell me about this?"

"It's the warrior symbol of protection. The nine points of the triangles each stand for noble Viking warrior virtues: industriousness, hospitality, discipline, honor, truth, courage, fidelity, self-reliance, and perseverance."

"I like that."

"What about yours?" I interlocked my fingers with hers and turned her arm over. The simple black tattoo ran from her left wrist to the middle of her forearm.

"We believe that we're born with a purpose and a destination. The path to that destination is the journey of life. The destination is the enlightenment. Most of us get lost, we struggle." She traced her tattoo. "It's called a unalome, which means reaching enlightenment. It's an ancient, spiritual symbol. The spiral and zigzags indicate my struggle with life. Eventually, I'll add a straight line when I find harmony."

"That's really squizz."

We were quiet for a while. I thought maybe she had fallen asleep, until she said, "The stars are brighter here. That cluster of six stars to our right, I can see that from Valinor just over the horizon at dusk. And that shape to our left is the planet, Zariah. I think we might be on Terronda."

"Are you trying to show off, Empress?" I teased.

"Maybe."

A hint of pink colored her cheek. I was glad she was finally talking. I knew she hated me. She had told me plenty of times. The way I betrayed her was not something easily forgiven—if ever. The silence was killing me though. I wanted to hear her voice, watch her eyes light up as she talked about something she loved. Revel in her animated expressions. I moved her hair off her neck and traced her marking. Slowly I pressed my lips to it and felt her body shiver. I wanted so much more, but instead I moved her hair back into place and buried my face in it. I couldn't get enough of her milk and honey scent.

I thought about what she said. Terronda? What did I know about that planet? "Terronda. Dangerous terrain, erratic weather, survivable, but difficult. Seems accurate. There's a settlement somewhere."

"And if we can get to that settlement, we can call for help."

<hr />

We got up at first light determined to make it across the ice. Not that either one of us had any clue how far it spanned.

"Ready?" I asked.

"No," she answered. "But we have no choice but to try, right?"

Truth was, there was no way that either of us could be ready for this. We didn't have the proper gear for cold weather. It didn't take long for Akacia to start shivering.

"Aren't you cold?" she asked.

"Yes." I wasn't as cold as she was apparently. In fact, I was surprised that it wasn't as cold as I thought it would be. Inhaling deeply, I released my breath, which formed in a white cloud.

The ice was beautiful, but deadly. One wrong move and we could die. The way the sun danced off the ice made me squint and I wished for sunshades.

The ice spikes got steeper and in some places we had to crawl over them. The cold that had seemed mild at first now whipped at my face and crept under my clothes. Oh, how I wished I had something hot to drink. Or to be wearing one of those protective suits to help with the temperature.

We walked sideways among the spikes. I shoved my foot into the snow, pressing down, making sure I had good footing. A deep, booming noise erupted and a cascade of white thundered down the mountain. We both fell backward, snow covering us. I began kicking immediately trying to get us out of there before we suffocated. The snow on top wasn't too deep and I burst through it. Taking deep breaths, I searched for Akacia. She had been right next to me. Using my already numb hands, I dug through the snow and grabbed her, pulling her free.

Her eyes were alight with fear and she was hyperventilating. "Breathe. You're safe."

"Can't..." she gasped, trembling from cold and panic.

I met her gaze and repeated, "Breathe." I took deep breaths to show her what I wanted her to do and soon her breathing stabilized.

We were both shivering now that our clothes were wet from the snow. Her lips were tinged with blue. We had to keep going. We couldn't stop. I took her hand in mine and pulled at her. "C'mon."

"Look," she said with chattering teeth and pointed when we finally made it over a high snowdrift. "Are th...those tr... trees?"

They were far in the distance, but I thought she was right. We could make it by nightfall if we hurried. I tugged her hand and forced her to continue on.

"I'm so cold, Ever." She slumped against the ice.

"I know. We have to keep going."

"Rest."

She was getting tired and hypothermic. I had to get us out of there. I couldn't let her die here. I needed to warm her up, but how would I do that quickly without anything?

"No. You can't. We can't. We have to keep going." I grabbed her and without thinking, pressed my lips against hers. The kiss was intense, filled with passion and fire. My heart beat hard and fast and I hoped hers was doing the same. She moaned into the heated kiss, pressed into me and our tongues met. Her hands were on my back, holding me against her. I was the first to pull away. If it weren't for the fact that we had to get out of the cold, I would have happily kissed her all day long.

"I need you to walk with me."

She nodded with eyes wider and more alert than they had been a moment before.

Before we continued on, I scooped some of the snow up in the bowl. Once it melted, we could drink it.

The ice thinned and soon our feet touched rock and then dirt. Akacia stumbled, but I grabbed her and held her up. We needed to get further from the ice. If we could make it to the trees, I could build a fire.

Arms wrapped around each other, we finally made it. We both fell to the ground at the edge of the tree line.

My body warmed quickly, but my hands were red and raw. Akacia was still shaking. I needed to get both of us warm. "I'll be right back," I told her and wandered into the forest to gather as many branches as I could. My hands were so cold that it took extra long to get the fire started. Both of us started to relax as we warmed up. I offered Akacia water first. She drank some and gave it back to me to finish.

Once I was toasty warm, I knew I needed to find us food. I set up a trap and looked around. I saw a plant that I knew grew nuts. Kneeling next to it, I pulled it out and brought it back to the fire.

The fire I built kept us warm. I wanted to talk to her. To hear her voice. Learn more about her. What she said before about not being able to move on circled in my head, filling me with regret. Maybe if I hadn't turned her over to Caspar, we would have had a shot. Maybe in another life. Still, I dreaded the moment that we would part because I knew she wasn't going to have anything to do with me once we were off this planet. So I might as well talk to her while I could. Though I wasn't sure why I was torturing myself.

"Tell me something."

Akacia turned to me and studied my face. I wasn't expecting her to respond, but she did. "Just something? Or something in particular?"

"Something interesting."

She poked the fire with a stick. "My life pales in comparison to yours."

TALIA JAGER

"I'm sure there's something." I handed her a few nuts.

"You would just call me privileged. I spent my childhood with parents who loved me. When they died, it fell to the counsel to raise me, teach me, and train me. Then when I was old enough, I took over."

"No special moments? No first love?"

She looked up and held my gaze. "No."

"What were your parents like?"

She laughed. "What I remember apparently isn't who they were."

"They must have loved you." I popped a few nuts in my mouth.

"I guess. I mean, they must have, right? To do something so crazy?" The fire danced in her eyes. "My mom was a good teacher. She was kind and patient. Everyone loved her. My dad was smart. He was confident and committed. I looked up to him."

"So he was the Emperor of Valinor?"

"Yes, but he was also a scientist. He was the head of Daystellar Research Incorporated. He loved science. Loved research…"

Her words faded into the background. Daystellar Research Incorporated…DRI. My mouth went dry. Those were the people responsible for…well, my whole life. Akacia's father was the head? It made sense, though. The experiments. Her nanites.

"What's wrong?"

"Nothing. I…uh…think I heard my trap going off." I stood up. "I'll be right back."

My mind filled with questions. How could the universe be so small? I had always imagined myself meeting the people behind DRI. Finding out more about the experiments. I had pictured a crazy old guy. It was also bizarre to find out he had a family, was the Emperor of a planet, and that the people loved him.

In the woods, I found a small animal in the trap. Quickly, I snapped its neck, filled my pockets with berries, and returned to the fire.

Akacia looked up as soon as I stepped out of the trees. Her eyes lit up at the sight of food in my hand. She didn't say anything else and I didn't offer an explanation as I skinned and cooked the animal.

I overcooked it a little, but it was food. We ate the nuts and berries with it. Afterward, I buried the bones.

"What about your parents?"

I looked up. "What?"

"You asked about mine. What about yours? What are they like?"

"I don't know," I answered honestly. She was watching me, waiting for me to say more. "They're smart, resourceful, kind people. At least I think they are. I was taken from my parents when I was young and trained on a ship. I don't remember much about my family. I know what they look like, but who they really are…I can't answer that. Everything I do, I do it for them."

She was satisfied with my answer and I was thankful for that. Talking to her was scarily easy. I wasn't used to it and I wasn't sure how much I should tell her. I didn't want her looking at me differently. More than anything I wanted a chance to make things right.

CHAPTER TWELVE

AKACIA

EVERLEIGH WAS BEHIND ME. HER arm over my waist. I felt safe. I didn't want to move, but when I opened my eyes, there was a small, gray animal with a long tail and five digits on each paw sitting in front of me, staring at me. It had big, round eyes, pointy ears that jutted out from his head, four small nubs—two above each eye, and a flat, pink nose.

It was by far the cutest thing I had ever seen, but then again looks could be deceiving. I nudged Everleigh. When she stirred, she let out a little groan.

"Look," I whispered.

"What's it doing?"

"Watching us. Think it's dangerous?"

"I don't know."

The little animal tilted its head, blinked and came a little closer. I stiffened unsure of what to expect. I reached out and grabbed a nut and handed it out to him. He took a few more steps and snatched it out of my hand.

"We need those," Everleigh said.

"He's cute."

He scurried around and found our pile of uneaten berries.

He shoved the berries in his mouth until his cheeks puffed out. I chuckled at him and it felt good. Something about seeing this little creature gave me hope. If he could survive out here, so could we.

We began our day with some nuts and a couple of those good smelling herbs. At least my breath wouldn't be horrid. My legs ached from walking for days. I was still tired and hungry, but I had begun to heal. I hadn't thought I could face Everleigh or talk to her again, or feel her lips on mine, but my heart was softening.

We were walking through a meadow with small hills and a lake. A large black cloud seemed to be heading toward us. Ever noticed it almost at the same time I did. Her eyebrows arched and she stopped walking. A bug flew by me, then another, and another. "Ow!" she shouted, slapping the back of her neck.

One of the bugs landed on my arm. It made a buzzing sound and then flew up an inch and rammed into me with its stinger. I whacked it, knocking it out of the air, but before its dead body even hit the ground, another one was on my neck and then one landed on my hand.

"We have to take cover." In the time it took Ever to look around, I had been stung two more times. Her eyes stopped on the lake. "We have to go under. Do you understand?" Her eyes searched mine as she waited for an answer. Another bug landed on her and stung her. She grimaced and flicked it off. "Akacia! They're coming! We have to go under!"

I started shaking my head. My eyes traveled from the water to the cloud of bugs still heading our way. We had been stung handfuls of times, but that would be nothing compared to if we were here when the rest of the bugs arrived. But what she was suggesting…going under the water…I shuddered.

"I won't let anything happen to you." Ever yanked on my hand dragging me to the water.

More bugs stung us as Ever pulled me deeper into the water. "We have to go under and stay there for a minute. I will hold onto you. You'll be safe."

She didn't wait any longer. She quickly spun me around so my back was to her chest, wrapped her arms around me, and she went under the water taking me with her.

Caspar's face filled my mind. Lorcan dragged me to the basin of water, grabbed me by the neck, and held me under. My lungs burned and I began to kick and thrash. Ever's hold on me slipped and I swam toward the surface. She grabbed my hands and pulled me close to her. Her eyes were wild and she shook her head. She pulled me to her and held me.

I was going to die.

Underwater.

Drowning on some crazy planet with the girl I wanted to spend forever with.

The girl who had betrayed me.

What kind of craziness was this? Maybe I was stuck in a coma somewhere and this was a dream.

Finally after what seemed like forever, she pushed us to the surface. I gasped for air, she hardly seemed out of breath. She scanned the area looking for the bugs. "They're gone. Are you okay?"

I didn't answer. I was still trying to catch my breath.

"Look in my eyes."

By now I knew what to do. I placed my hand on her chest and matched her breath for breath.

"Good," she said when my breathing finally evened. With my hand in hers, she led me out of the water. We sank onto the grass and I examined the places on my arms that burned. Welts had formed where the bugs had stung us.

"Come on. We'll find a place to camp and dry off."

Ever helped me to my feet and we walked a little farther until we found a good place to spend the night.

After the fire was made she disappeared into the woods to find dinner and I laid out our clothes so they could dry. I sat on a rock with the blanket over me, staring out at the lake, wondering how I was ever going to be okay again.

She came back with another of those small animals she'd caught before and more berries. As she cooked the food, I slipped away to the forest and found some herbs to make a paste for our stings.

After eating, I applied the paste to the welts all over my body. It soothed the pain. Then I gestured for Everleigh to sit down and I did the same for her.

"Sorry I froze."

"I understand," she replied.

We rested for the night and got started walking again at first light. I was a little edgy from the stings and being underwater again, so when the dark clouds began rolling in that afternoon, I panicked.

"It's just a storm," Ever said.

Without warning lightning struck way too close and I let out a yip. We picked up the pace. Another lightning strike hit the ground behind us. Pea-sized hail started pelting down, stinging our already raw skin.

"Look." It was the little animal from the other morning. He had followed us and was now running toward some large boulders. "Follow him."

Lightning hit so close the hairs on my arms stood up. We skidded to the boulder and hid in between two of them.

Something tickled me and I squealed. The little animal popped up on my shoulder. Everleigh shot me a look. "I guess he likes us?"

She put out the bowl to catch run off and we drank every time it filled up.

The lightning storm didn't last too much longer. We climbed out of our hiding spot and continued on.

<hr />

For two more nights, we walked through the trees with our little friend following us. We gathered nuts and berries and Ever usually got lucky enough to catch something. We found a small stream for water on the second day and though it wasn't deep enough to bathe in, we both washed up.

Staring at the fire one night, the little animal came over and curled up in between my feet. I reached down and scratched his head. "I'm going to call you Nero."

Ever was at the stream collecting water while I played with Nero on one of our breaks when the air was suddenly pierced by her screams.

"Akacia!" she screamed my name and ran faster than humanly possible toward me. I heard a noise behind me just as Nero jumped onto my leg and held on. I spun around to find two large, gray beasts coming right at me.

My eyes grew wide and I searched for my spear. Both hers and mine were too far away for me to get to in time. I reached for my knife as one grabbed at me. I kept the furless, human-like creature with black, feral eyes at arm's length. It was strong, but so was I. The second one was only inches away. I could deal with one, not two. Ever fired repeatedly at one until he jerked back and fell to the ground. I plunged my dagger into the one in front of me. Its mouth opened and it shrieked in pain. I had never seen so many teeth inside something that looked close to human.

It seemed more irritated by being stabbed than it was hurt and it started coming after me again. He knocked me over and ripped into Ever's leg. Screaming I threw myself on him shoving the knife in over and over until he finally fell to the ground.

Out of breath, I flopped onto the ground and closed my eyes. "Ever? You okay?" She didn't answer. "Shit." I crawled over to her. "Everleigh!"

She turned her head and looked my way. "I'm alive."

"What's wrong?"

"My leg."

I looked where she gestured. The beast had left a ragged set of teeth marks in her leg.

"That good, huh?"

My eyes met hers. "You'll be fine."

"You don't know that."

"It's just a bite."

"What if it makes me turn into one of them?"

"You mean like a vampire or zombie?"

"Yeah." She was being completely serious.

"That stuff's not real. Those are just things people used to write books about."

"Stories had to come from somewhere."

"Ever. You're not going to turn into one of these things."

I took the one blanket we had been carrying with us, dipped it into stream, and then carefully cleaned her wound. It wasn't bleeding much, so I didn't need to cauterize it. I wrapped the cloth tightly around it. "I need to find some herbs." I looked in her eyes. "Are you sure you're okay?"

"Wishing I could heal like you."

My eyebrows arched. "Do you think I could give you some of my blood?"

"No," she said quickly. Too quickly. Maybe she really did think I was a freak. "No. Just find the herbs."

I hurried into the woods. My schooling had taught me a lot about plants, herbs, and healing, not only for Valinor but for other planets as well. I could only hope that it would apply on this planet. A little chitter caught my attention. Nero had followed me. He was scampering around to different plants like he knew what I was looking for. He stopped at one plant and chittered a little bit louder.

"Yeah, that looks like one. Good job," I said then gave him a good rub behind the ears. I found two more I thought would be helpful and ran back to Ever. She had maneuvered herself up against a tree. Using the bowl, I ground up the herbs and mixed with water to make a paste. After unraveling the cloth, I scooped up the paste and smeared it all over the bite. She winced. "Sorry." I wrapped it back up and then took the last herb. "Eat it," I ordered. "You're not going to be able to walk on that leg."

"I can do it."

"Stop being ridiculous."

She let out a sigh. "Okay, I'll rest overnight and we can try in the morning."

I nodded, knowing that there was no way she was going to be able to trek on with this injury. "Let's move away from the beasts a little and we'll rest there."

We moved down the stream some so we didn't have to look at the bodies. Then I gathered the necessary things to build a fire and within minutes had a flame going.

"Hmm," Ever hummed, as if she were surprised.

"I might be the Empress, but they teach me all the skills too."

She cracked a smile. "Good."

"You have a beautiful smile."

Her cheeks tinted a lovely shade of pink.

Instead of waiting until one of us had a nightmare, I gestured to the ground. Her eyes widened with surprise. She laid down first and I spooned her. Having her so close felt as right as it always did. I pressed my lips to the spot behind her ear and made my way down the side of her neck as I pulled her in a bit closer.

"I'm a Splicer," she said, letting out a long, shuddering breath.

My hand froze. "A what?"

"Your father wasn't just dabbling in nanites. He was making cutting edge breakthroughs in many different areas. Your father created the Splicers."

This was the second time I'd heard that word. "I'm not sure what you mean. Like a species?"

She scoffed. "Hardly. There aren't a lot of us."

Suddenly images flashed in my mind from when I was on Caspar's spacecraft. This is what he wanted. Information about Splicers. "Caspar…he questioned me about this."

"Did he tell you what Splicers are?"

The memory was hazy. "He said my father took predator animal DNA and did something with it."

"They wanted to create better warriors. So they asked for volunteers to have their DNA spliced with that of a predator animal. It was their job to have children, called Second Generation Splicers. These kids were supposed to be protected and trained until they were old enough to be warriors and guards. Instead, the children were kidnapped."

Something in me clicked. "SGS. Second Generation Splicers. I remember when my parents were killed, people kept talking about SGS. I didn't know what it meant then and nobody has brought it up since." I grew quiet for another minute. "Caspar wanted to know about my father's research."

"Caspar is the one who stole us from our families. He keeps our families on a planet somewhere and as long as we're working for him, they stay alive and taken care of. He has been trying to replicate your father's work for years. That must be why he wanted you. To find his research."

"I know nothing about his research. Nothing at all. I was a kid. Nobody's ever talked to me about it."

The information about what my father became less important when I focused on what she was saying. She was a Splicer. Her DNA was joined with some animal DNA.

Her head turned without warning. "Are you afraid of me now?" she asked in a whisper. Her gold eyes met mine.

"What? No. I'm not afraid." I wiped the tears from her cheeks. "Intrigued. What were you spliced with?"

"Jaguar. I can run fast. I am strong and have good reflexes. It's why I wasn't as cold as you in the snow and why I caught you when your foot slipped. I hear better than any humanoid, see better, smell better—"

"Beautiful," I whispered, tangling my hands into the soft hair at the nape of her neck.

Slowly, like we were magnetically drawn to one another our mouths drifted together. I tentatively pressed my lips to hers, then unsure, I pulled back to judge her expression. She was smiling. There was nothing tentative about the second kiss. It was passionate and sure. The kiss deepened immediately and I knew it would leave me with bruised lips, but I couldn't stop. Her lips parted and I took that as an invitation that left our tongues playing together.

When we finally pulled away, both breathless, we stared at each other for a minute. If we weren't stuck on a foreign planet, hungry and tired, and she wasn't injured, I would have liked it to go much further.

"Thank you," I said.

Her brow furrowed. "For?"

"Telling me. I know opening up isn't easy for you."

"You make it easy." She ran her thumb over my lips. "Can we sleep like this tonight?"

Kissing her thumb, I answered, "Yeah."

I stayed awake as long as I could staring into her eyes. When I woke, we were tangled up in each other, and it was by far the best feeling in the galaxy. But as my eyes focused on her, I realized something was wrong. Her coloring wasn't good and her breathing was labored. I put my hand to her forehead. She was hot. This wasn't good. The beast's bite must have venom in it.

I sat up and examined her wound. It was red and pus leaked out. "Ever?"

She stirred and slowly opened her eyes. "Kaci." Her voice was weak and by the look in her eyes I could tell she knew something was wrong. "If I turn into...one of them...kill me."

"Ever..."

"Promise?"

It was obvious she needed to hear it. "Promise."

"Thank you."

"I have to think." I paced around the fire, turning away

from her, so she wouldn't see the fear in my eyes. When I turned back, her eyes were closed and Nero was cuddled up next to her.

I knelt down beside her and straightened the blanket. Her eyes fluttered open again. "I'm going to find something to help you."

Her hand shot out and grabbed mine. "Don't go."

"I'll be back. I need you to stay alive."

"I'll try."

"No. I want a promise."

She gave me a slight smile. "Promise."

I kissed her forehead and then took off into the forest.

CHAPTER THIRTEEN

AKACIA

THE VENOM WAS KILLING EVERLEIGH. That much I knew. I didn't know how to stop its effects and or how long she'd live.

Something chattered behind me. I turned and found Nero following. Kneeling down, I said, "You want to come? I need to find something to help Ever." I wiped the tears off my cheeks with the back of my hand. "I have to help her."

Nero jumped on my shoulder and I continued through the forest, trying to find anything I could use. It wasn't just an infection. This was venom from some freaky beast. How was I going to cure that?

I combed through plants, trying to find something that might work.

A bolt of lightning struck nearby. "You've got to be kidding me," I mumbled.

That was all that I needed. I shrunk down next to a tree while the storm boomed around me. I watched the way it was going, worried about Everleigh, and was relieved that it wasn't headed toward her. When it was done, Nero hopped off my shoulder and ran ahead. "Hey! Nero! Come back!" I chased after him.

Suddenly I found myself surrounded by wet, glowing fungus-like organism. Nero ran around in a circle and then back to me.

"Are you trying to tell me that this will help her?" I asked him like he was going to answer me which was ridiculous. But it was even more ridiculous that he chittered like he actually was answering me. I nodded, rubbed his head, and began collecting the glowing stuff.

Snarling sounds brought my hands to a stop. I looked up and through the trees. Four beasts chased a large four-legged animal through the woods. I considered my options. I could stay where I was and hope they wouldn't find me. I could run and hope they wouldn't notice. But if they did, I'd lead them back to Ever and she couldn't fight back. I looked up. I could climb. Get in the tree and wait for them to go.

That was what I had to do.

Quietly, I climbed up high enough to be hidden. Nero sat with me and we waited. The beasts attacked the animal with a vengeance. My stomach clenched at the sight and I looked away. We waited there for too long while they ate. Maybe I should have run? What if she died while I was up in this freaking tree?

Tears slid my face and I clamped my mouth shut so the beasts wouldn't hear me. Nero buried himself in my chest like he knew what I was thinking.

Finally the beasts finished. My breath hitched when it looked like they were going to head toward Ever, but something caught their attention and they took off the other way.

I climbed out of the tree, finished collecting the glowing fungus, and raced through the forest back to camp. My heart thudded in my chest the closer I got and almost stopped when I saw her. Ever's color was grayish and she didn't look like she was breathing.

No.

I rushed to her and fell to the ground. I put my hand on her chest and released a breath when I felt her exhale. I took all the glowing fungus-like stuff and piled it in front of me.

"Ever? I'm here. I've got the stuff." Having no idea what I should do with the fungus, I decided to do it all. First, I opened her mouth and shoved some in.

Then, grabbing the bowl, I took off to the stream, filled it with water and hurried back. I dribbled a little in her mouth. I mixed some of the fungus into the water and poured as much as I could down her throat. After getting more water, I made up a paste and smothered it on top of the bite.

That was all I could do. I sat down and held her hand. Nothing seemed to happen. No quick miracle cure.

"Don't die. I forgive you. I wanted to hate you, but instead I fell in love with you. So please don't die."

The words surprised me, but they were the truth. I loved her. I was mad at her for what she'd done to me. Unbelievably mad, but I loved her. Didn't you forgive the ones you loved?

Night fell and Ever didn't die, although she came very close. She did take an extremely long time to recover. Her color seemed a little better and when I couldn't keep my eyes open any longer, I lay next to her and let them close.

I woke before daylight and put more paste on the wound. Her coloring was normal and her fever gone. She stirred and her eyes fluttered open.

"Hey," I whispered.

"You saved me. You could have left me, but you didn't."

My eyes were wet. "Of course, I saved you."

"Why?"

Because I love you. "You saved me. Now we're even. I told you that you wouldn't turn into one of them."

"I'm glad you were right."

"Me too. Then I wouldn't get to do this." I leaned forward and captured her warm lips. The kiss was soft, yet deep and demanding. She made a noise, part whimper, part moan. I pulled on her bottom lip with my teeth before pushing my tongue into her mouth. My heart was hammering so hard I wondered if she could hear it. I didn't want to overdo it because she still needed to recover, so I pulled away leaving a wide grin on her face.

CHAPTER FOURTEEN

EVERLEIGH

THE VENOM WAS GONE OR neutralized or whatever, but my leg was still injured and I was weak. We decided to stay where we were for another night.

During the day, Akacia did all the things that I had done since we crashed here. She was just as capable as I was of surviving. I had jumped into being the leader because she was royalty and I didn't think she knew what to do. Boy, had I been stupid.

Telling Akacia everything was more than a little difficult for me, but I was glad to have done it. At first I wasn't sure how she would handle it, but she barely blinked an eye. It was like it didn't matter to her at all to learn that I had animal DNA in me. That fact alone would scare off most people. Throw in that I had been abducted and worked for a bad man, she should be running far away. But she stayed.

Akacia was lying on her back looking up at the clouds. "That one looks like a face," she said, pointing.

"What?"

"The clouds. They take shapes. You just have to use your imagination to see what they are. Try."

I looked up at the clouds in the orange sky. "They're clouds. Puffy, white clouds."

"Look further." She pointed at one. "It's a heart."

I looked at where she pointed and maybe, if I squinted just the right way, I could see a heart. I was so used to being in space, that seeing clouds from below was weird. Either that or I lacked an imagination. Maybe both.

"Tell me more about your travels," she said.

"Like what?"

"Where have you gone? What have you seen?"

I started off telling her about flying the ship around the universe. How I'd seen hundreds of stars and planets. The different space stations that I had visited. I told her about meeting new people and how no two places were the same. How everything was different and mysterious. "Sometimes we go down to a planet to explore it. See what resources it offers. There have been times where we find awesome ones and times that were downright scary."

"Scary?"

"Pools of lava with out of control, shooting lava balls. A planet with an atmosphere so green you can see the poisons lingering. Ground like quicksand that sucks you in so fast, you don't have time to scream."

Her eyes were wide in horror. I felt a little guilty.

"There are beautiful planets, too. Those with colors you never knew existed. Foods you never knew could taste so good. Meadows filled with the most beautiful flowers."

"You've seen so much."

"I never get to spend a lot of time at these places though."

"Because of Caspar?"

"Yes."

"So you do all these jobs for him and in turn he lets your family live?"

I nodded.

"You rescued me. You went against him." Her blue eyes bore into mine. "Your family—"

"Probably dead."

She closed her eyes and when she opened them again, they were wet. "Why? Why did you come for me?"

All the feelings that I felt for her came rushing at me. "Because...because you're you."

Her breath hitched.

"When we get off this planet, what will happen?" she asked.

"I'll get you home."

"What will happen to *you*?"

I looked back at the clouds. "A bear."

She followed my gaze. "I'm not letting it go."

"He'll kill me." I sighed, not wanting to think about it, but not wanting to keep anything from her either. "He's probably killed my family, my crew, and their families. If he finds me, he'll kill me."

"So we have to kill him first."

My eyes darted back to her. "No. There's no 'we' in this."

"Like hell there isn't." She sat up and pulled me toward her with a sense of urgency. Her eyes flashed with anger and despair. Not waiting a second longer, her mouth crashed down on mine. I couldn't hold back and let myself succumb to her kiss.

Vulnerable.

I was vulnerable in her arms.

Yet, I felt safe.

She made me feel safe and loved. Something I had never

felt before. My eyes pricked with tears and my chest swelled to the point of bursting.

I had figured out her tells. When her hand was tangled in the back of my hair, like it was right now, she was trying to figure out what to do next. I took the lead, moving my lips to her neck, under her ear, over to the dimple on her cheek, and then back to her mouth. My hand slipped under her shirt and she gasped at the feel of my skin against hers. The kisses were long and slow, as if we had all the time in the world to do nothing more than kiss.

She pulled away, a little out of breath, and said, "Tell me again, how there's no 'we' in this."

"Kaci…"

Her face lit up in a wide smile.

"What?"

"I love it when you say my name."

"Kaci," I said again. "I just got done saving you. I'm not putting you in harm's way again."

"Ever, you're the reason he had me in the first place. I still struggle with that. With my feelings. But, there's one thing I know, he'll never stop coming after either of us as long as he's alive."

"There's nothing we can do about it right now." If we did make it off this planet, then I needed to get her safe, and go after Caspar myself. I needed revenge for everything that he's done. I was done with being his slave.

I lay in between her legs that evening with the stupid monkey-like animal curled up in my lap. I almost brushed him off, but

Akacia made some 'aw' sound and it melted my heart a little. She was becoming attached, naming him and all.

She traced my eyebrows, my ear, and then down my jawbone. "How did you get this scar?"

I ran my finger over it. "Caspar."

"In training?" she guessed.

"No." It wasn't a pleasant memory.

"If it's too personal—"

"He marked me so I wasn't beautiful, so I'd fear him, so I knew I belonged to him. He wanted to tame me, but he couldn't. He couldn't break me. He thought that since he had us so young, we'd be loyal to him. I was stubborn, so he tried to disfigure me. When that didn't work, he killed my best friend, and threatened my parents. I finally agreed to do what he wanted. It used to be worse, thicker, and red. He even clipped off part of my ear lobe." I touched my lobe, which was normal looking now. "I had some treatments done that have helped heal it."

She was quiet for a minute and I wondered what she was thinking. Then she leaned down and kissed my ear and the scar. "A scar doesn't make you ugly or make you belong to someone. What about the rest of your crew? They seem loyal to you."

"Briar pretended to be loyal to Caspar from early on. Hux and Zabe, they were loyal to him at first, but within a few months of being with us, we changed their thinking. We still did what Caspar wanted because he threated the lives of our loved ones, but we were one with our hate for him." I pushed the memory to the far back of my mind. "Tell me about your days."

"My days?" She looked confused.

"What do you do all day? What is the job of an Empress?"

She ran her fingers along my arm. "Though I am an Empress, I don't live in a castle nor was I pampered."

I raised my eyebrows and opened my mouth to make a comment, but she stared me down. "Yes, I had a chef and someone to make my clothes. I didn't want for anything, other than my parents and freedom."

It didn't get past me that we both yearned for the same things.

"We don't have balls or fancy parties. I don't dress in frilly, poofy dresses. I have a crown I only wear to ceremonies when I go off-planet. Well, I guess I should say I *had* a crown. It was lost on Caipra." She blinked back tears. "It had been passed down from my great-great-grandmother, Malou. I told you how I was hidden away after my parents were killed. My friend, Bristow, was as well. We grew up together, learned together, trained together. He's my family. They trained us in everything. How to live off the land. How to fight. How to grow food. Plus all the math, science, and universe history someone could handle. Every once in a while we were allowed to go into the forest through a secret tunnel to practice our survival skills. When I was older, they finally brought me out of hiding. I met the people of Valinor, no longer a child, but an Empress. I promised them safety and a happy, prospering place to live. I promised equality for all, no matter what. We're peaceful. The people have freedom to live as they choose. It's not about who has the best job or the most money. Mostly we don't deal in money at all. They trade with each other and take care of each other." She looked down at me. "Don't look at me like that."

"Like what?"

"All cynical. This is how we live. It works. Our population isn't huge. We don't have countries spread all over our world.

This is why others have wanted my planet. They want the resources we have and they want to turn it into a money making machine. I won't allow that."

"If they think you're dead…"

I heard her swallow. "It could be bad if another administration has found out, they could attack. I'm hoping they put Bristow in charge. He's prepared. But I know that's not what he wants. He wants to explore, like you. What scares me the most…I hope I have a home to go home to."

"We'll get you home."

She sighed, lost in her thoughts for a few minutes. "I read a lot while in hiding. They were the only adventures I got to go on. What about you? When you're not kidnapping Empresses?"

"You happen to the be the only Empress I've ever kidnapped." I looked back at her.

"Really?" She bit down on her lip to hide the smile that was growing on her face.

"Honest. We cruise around exploring when we're not on jobs for Caspar."

"Sounds so adventurous. Tell me about your favorite adventure."

"I once visited a planet that had weak gravity. If you walked carefully, you could stay on the ground, but if you moved fast or jumped, up you'd go. We had a lot of fun just playing on that planet. We weren't there to play though. We had heard about a cave full of glowing treasure, so we set out to find it."

She stared at me with wide, curious eyes.

"The planet had little darkness, so our sleeping patterns were off. We were there for five of their days though before we found it. And it was magnificent," I recalled the beautiful rocks and gems that were in the cave, all of them glowing. "We each took one and we left the cave. We've never told anybody where it was. It was so breathtaking we didn't want it destroyed."

"What does Caspar have you do?"

"Usually we steal for him. Sometimes he'll have us spy or plant something."

We were quiet for a while. Her fingers traced the jaguar design on my arm.

"Have you ever been in love?" she asked.

My heart banged in my chest. "No."

"Never?"

"I've had…relationships, not even sure that's the right word, but never been…" I cleared my throat. "No."

"Relationships. Tell me about them."

"Really?"

"You have something better to do?" she asked.

"Well…no."

"Then spill."

"I don't do serious. I can't. I guess you could say I have one night stands."

"Because of Caspar?"

Letting out a long breath, I confirmed what she had already assumed. "I can't love someone when he owns me."

"Tomorrow isn't promised," she said. "You should live life to the fullest. Without hesitation."

It wasn't the first time she said that. It was a good motto. One that I wish I could adopt. But that couldn't be how I lived. Because of Caspar. Because of the Authority. Whoever I fell in love with would be in danger in one way or the other. I couldn't do that to anyone. Couldn't do that to her.

That night, Akacia woke up screaming. I reached out to her, wanting to pull her close, but she pushed me away. Tears streamed down her face, but she wouldn't even look at me. I wondered if the nightmare was about me. My heart felt like a brick in my chest. She didn't talk about it, not then, not in the morning. When I woke, she had already brought me food, and was ready to clean the wound.

I didn't talk, didn't ask about the nightmare. I just let her do what needed to be done.

"Try to stand up." She grabbed me under one arm and helped me up.

Carefully, I put weight on my leg. It hurt, but it wasn't excruciating. I took a few steps. "I'll be fine, but slow."

"Would you rather stay here another day or two?"

The past two days had been nice. I almost wished we could stay for good. We could build a house, plant some food, and be together. Nobody trying to kill us. Nobody to answer to. Nobody to take care of but us. But that was a fantasy.

"Ever?"

I shook myself out of my daydream. "We can go."

"What were you thinking about?"

"Staying here." Ignoring the curious and confused look she gave me, I grabbed my spear. Not waiting for her to say anything else, I started walking. Nero followed, running between her and me, twittering.

The walk was difficult with my injured leg. We had to rest a lot, which was okay with me. I felt like it made the journey longer and as long as no more of those monsters attacked, I didn't mind and she didn't seem to either.

"Tell me the story behind the jaguar tattoo that you have," she asked after we set out the next morning. "I assume that's what it is."

"Yes." I ran my hand over my arm. "It's a part of who I am. Something in me wanted to express it somehow."

"I like how you chose to do that. Are you all jaguars?"

"Who? My crew?"

"Yeah."

"No, but you'll have to ask them. We made a pact not to talk about each other to anyone else." I stopped, thinking about my crew. "I know they're probably dead, but I don't feel comfortable spilling their secrets." I peeked over at her. "Sorry."

"It's okay. I respect that."

By mid-afternoon, another change in the landscape occurred. Trees vanished and fields started to spread across the lands to both sides. I thought I could see the hint of a city in the distance. If we hurried, we could reach it by nightfall.

Akacia stood next to me. "Ready to get off this planet?"

I didn't respond.

She started walking.

"Wait!" I called after her. She turned around and looked at me with those big blue eyes of hers. "Do you think we could take one more night?"

Her face lit up. "Yeah." She looked around and then pointed. "We can stay over there."

While I set a trap, Akacia gathered twigs and built a fire. The wind blew, tousling her hair and leaving a strand in her face. I desperately wanted to reach over and brush it to the side. She was so beautiful. I just wanted to touch her, kiss her, and claim her as my own. I had no idea if she'd even let me, but damn, I wanted to.

"You told me what you have to do, but what do you like to do?" I inquired, wanting to hear her voice longer.

"I don't get a lot of free time."

"You must enjoy something."

She quirked her mouth to the side as she thought. It was one of my favorite expressions of hers. Just after the way she looked at me before we kiss. "I like the way the dirt feels in my hands when I'm planting. I like the way whatever weapon I'm using becomes a part of me. I like making up stories of exploring the universe. I like singing, though I'm not very good at it. And I like animals." She looked at Nero.

"I would like to hear you sing, even if you're not good. What's your favorite color?"

"Gold," she answered quickly. I smiled and started to say something about her color choice, but she interrupted me. "What do you like to do?"

"I like adventure. I like traveling and doing things. I like riding horses and feeling the wind in my hair and diving underwater looking for treasure. I like playing truth or dare—I always choose dares. I also like sitting around with my friends playing a game of cards and getting a massage at the space station."

She nodded and "hmm'd" like she was storing all that information somewhere.

After eating, Nero ran up and down a tree until he got tired and then crashed in Kaci's lap. She stroked him and I felt a pang of jealousy in my chest. Rolling my eyes, I laughed inwardly. I was jealous of an animal.

Night fell and we stoked the fire. She started singing a song I didn't know. Her voice was raw and beautiful and just for me. Well, maybe Nero too.

"See?" she said when she was done. "Nothing to write home about."

Rolling my eyes, I leaned over and seized her lips. She let out a moan and kissed me back with the same intense response. Without really thinking about it, I grabbed her hand and scooted backward until I was against the tree. Pulling her to me, she straddled me. I held her away from me for a moment and just looked at her.

She had the most amazing smile on her lips and her eyes were so vivid. Her beautiful curves, her ample breasts, all of her beckoned me. With my thumb, I traced from her ear down her jawline, and placed it on her neck feeling the steady thrum of her pulse.

Kaci's eyes seemed to beg as she licked her lips and looked at my lips. I kissed her neck and she arched her back. My hands found the small of her back and pulled her closer, eliminating any space left between us. I lifted my face to hers and she brushed her lips across mine sending a shudder all the way through my body. Our lips crashed together again with a surge of fire. Her fingers brushed over my cheeks, down to my neck, and finally tangled in my hair.

She pulled away leaving me breathless and wanting more. I lifted my head up again to meet her lips, but she smiled avoiding me and trailed kisses from my neck down to my shoulder.

As much as I wanted to be with her in every possible way, I didn't want it to be out in the middle of nowhere with a bum leg. I think she understood that too because after a few more kisses, she turned around and settled down in between my legs for the night.

Morning came quickly. When I woke, I realized Kaci hadn't woken up with a nightmare. I kissed her neck. My heart picked up pace when she let out a low moan. I didn't want to get up. Didn't want to start walking. Didn't want to find out what was in that city. I just wanted to stay here, with her.

"Guess we should start the last leg of our journey. We should be on the way home by nightfall," she said. Her tone of voice was somewhat sad and I couldn't help but think she might be having some of the same thoughts.

I didn't know what would happen when we got off this planet, but I feared that once she was safe, her feelings about me would change. I didn't want to have hope. I didn't deserve it.

We began our trek to our destination when I noticed something in the ground up ahead. Once my brain realized what I was looking at, I grabbed her arm. "Stop!"

"What?"

"Look." I pointed to the field in front of us. There were pieces of bodies scattered throughout.

"Are those the beasts that have been attacking us?"

My eyes scanned the area. "I think so. I think it's a minefield."

She blew out a long breath. "How do we get across then?"

"I don't think we can. We need to figure out how to set them off."

Kaci was quiet while she stroked Nero's head. "Bristow and I skip stones in the lake. What if we throw rocks?"

"We could do that, but it'll take time and make a lot of noise. They'll know we're coming."

"Any other ideas?"

I picked up a rock and threw it as far as I could. It landed silently and I released a breath I didn't know I had been holding. We both gathered big rocks and first started rolling them and then throwing them.

"We'll have to take a few steps at a time to be far enough from a blast if we trigger one."

"Okay."

"Follow exactly in my footsteps."

"Why do you get to go first?"

I stared at her. "I can only hope I'm fast enough to get us out of the way if one goes off too close."

She studied me for a minute, but then nodded. She was rubbing her wrist, one of her nervous ticks.

For what seemed like the entire day, we carefully picked our way through the field trying to set off any bombs. Three went off before we reached the city limits.

CHAPTER FIFTEEN

AKACIA

THE STONE CITY BEFORE US was surrounded by water. It didn't have tall buildings or skyscrapers, but it did have two towers. My guess was they were lookout towers to see what was coming. I wondered how long they had been watching us and why they didn't come to our aid. It left a bad taste in my mouth.

Ever asked the question I was thinking, "Do you think they're trying to keep people in or something out?"

"I don't know."

"How do we get in?"

"There must be a way." I spun around. "Look at the fields. They're for farming."

"So we circle around the city and find it."

"Okay."

We were almost at the water when Nero started running around in circles and then took off to the left.

"Dumb thing." Everleigh sighed.

I stared at him for a minute. "I think he wants to show us something." I followed him to a tunnel leading under the water. "Looks like that's the way in."

Concern darkened her eyes. "Maybe there's another way?"

I studied her face. "Are you scared?"

"No." She narrowed her eyes.

I raised my eyebrows.

"Maybe a little."

She looked adorable nibbling nervously on her lower lip. She was so badass, and yet she had a phobia. I wanted to wrap my arms around her and protect her from whatever it was she was afraid of.

"It's the only way home."

She fiddled with the button on her pants. "I know."

I walked to the tunnel entrance and then turned to look behind me. She hadn't moved a step. I held out my hand. "Come on. I've got you."

Slowly, like each step was a death sentence, she closed the space between us. She looked at my hand and then took it. Our fingers fit together perfectly. The darker it got, the harder Ever gripped my hand. I didn't think she was scared of the dark or the water, so I was guessing it was either being underground or small spaces. I didn't ask though. I'd let her open up when she was ready.

It was pitch black in there and even I began to get creeped out after a while. There was a tiny pinprick of light very far away that I headed for. I hoped it was the right way to go.

"Could you talk to me?" Ever asked.

I smiled. "Sure. About what?"

"Anything. I don't care."

"What do you think is in the city?"

"I don't know."

Laughing, I said, "Well, if you want to talk, we both have to use words."

"Okay. What do you think is in the city?"

"Hopefully people. And hopefully they have some technology so we can contact our homes. Food would be good. Really good food. And lots of water."

"A soft bed with a nice blanket."

"Yes."

"You said 'homes'."

"What?"

"You said you hoped we could contact our homes. I don't have one. The Nirvana was my home."

"We'll figure it out," I said. I wanted to invite her home with me, but there was still a part of me that didn't trust her. The betrayal ran deep and I was still healing. Would I ever be able to trust her enough to have a relationship with her? Would she want to stay on Valinor with me? Or would she want to be exploring? Too many questions, ones that I didn't know if I should ask and I didn't want to know the answers to some of the others.

"Kaci?"

"Hmm?"

"I can tell the mood changed even if I can't see your face."

"Just stuck in my head."

She grew quiet probably guessing what I was thinking. "What are you going to do with Nero?"

"I don't know."

"You know, to talk, it requires words."

I laughed. "Yes, it does. I want to keep him."

"I guessed that."

"The light is getting closer. We'll be there soon."

"I don't like tight spots," she admitted finally.

"I don't particularly like them either."

Ever gripped my hand hard and dragged me to a stop. "Something is coming," she whispered.

"What?"

"I can hear them. They're coming from that way." She gestured in front of us.

I glanced behind us wondering if we should go back. What if they were beasts or something worse? Before I could decide, someone yelled, "Stop!"

Bright lights shone in our faces. "Drop the weapons!"

We let the spears fall out of our hands.

"Hands out!" another voice followed.

Large guards wearing dark green uniforms surrounded us with their weapons aimed. I dropped Ever's hand and put both of mine out in front of me. One of the men with brown hair and a long beard stepped up to us and examined our hands. Raising a gun at my head, he said, "Who are you?"

"I'm Akacia Sparks, Empress of Valinor. We crashed on your planet about fifteen nights ago. We're not here to harm anyone. We just want to go home."

He was quiet for a long moment. His eyes moved to Ever and he said, "Who are you?"

"She's with me," I said. It was hard to explain why the sudden urge to protect Ever rose up in me after what she had done to me. It just felt like the right thing to do. I hoped she wouldn't make me regret it. "Do you have a communication device we could use?"

He grunted, turned, and began walking away. Just as I was about to call out to him, the other guards closed in on us and forced us to follow the bearded man.

"Where do you think they're taking us?" Ever asked.

"Would it be too optimistic to say the comms room?" I answered.

We emerged from the tunnel back into the bright light of the sun. The buildings were built out of different colored stones. It looked like homes were one color and government another, maybe businesses were the third color? The city wasn't large, but it was full of people who stopped and stared at us as we walked by. It reminded me a lot of where I lived, but Baile was more spread out.

We were led into one tan stone building and down a hall. A door opened and the guard pointed for us to go inside. After taking a deep breath, I entered pulling Ever behind me. The guard followed and the door closed. It was a small room with a table and chairs. Guess they weren't rolling out the red carpet for us.

"Please hand us everything on your bodies."

"Why?"

"We can't have you attacking us."

I took off my holster and handed it over. I didn't have anything else.

Ever refused to give them anything, so they took everything. Her guns, her knives, and her jump device. Before he left, he grabbed Nero off my shoulder.

"Pets, too."

"Hey!"

"We'll keep him alive." The guard glared at us.

The door opened and two men and a woman walked in. The men stood to the side, while the woman with long auburn hair and thin stern lips sat down and gestured for us to do the same.

"It's unusual for us to have visitors. I hope you'll excuse

the rude welcome," the lady said. "My name is Mellie. I am the leader of Terronda. You certainly got our attention crossing the minefield. We'll have to go plant some more."

"They protect you from the beasts?"

"Yes. We surrounded our city with bombs to keep the Grimelings out. They are not smart, but they are strong and unrelenting." She sat back. "One of our guards said you claim to be the Empress of Valinor, is that correct?"

"Yes. Could you contact Valinor and let them know? They will send rescue."

"How did you get here?" She didn't answer my question.

"We crashed."

"How?"

"I don't really know. Ship malfunction or something." I didn't want to give out the information that there were people after us, that we had been attacked.

The man on Mellie's left crinkled his forehead.

"And her?" Mellie asked.

"She's my bodyguard," I lied.

"Please, stay here. We're going to verify your story." Mellie stood and left the room.

Looking as the two guards took their positions outside the door, I said, "They're not letting us leave anyway."

"I don't like this. Something isn't right," Ever said.

"I know," I answered, reaching over and taking her hands in mine. "It can't be worse here, right?"

Her golden eyes met mine. She leaned close and said, "Keep our secrets."

I answered her with a nod. There was no way I was telling anyone here about my nanites or Ever's DNA.

The silence engulfed us as we sat at the table wondering

what our fate might be. Maybe we should have stayed in the wild. Built a house? Tried to survive among the monsters and crazy weather? No use fretting about it. We couldn't change any of that now.

Mellie returned. The guards followed. "Terronda is a beautiful planet. We are thankful for what we have here, but you've seen some of what we're up against. Erratic weather and strong beasts. Our winters are brutal. We barely have enough food to get through it." She leaned forward. "We have verified your identities. We will hold you here until we are paid for your safe return."

"You're ransoming us?" My hands balled into fists.

"Yes. We discovered that both of you have multiple people searching for you. Empress, while Valinor is looking for you, so is someone called Caspar. And you, Everleigh of the Nirvana, along with this Caspar person, you are wanted by the Authority."

"Bloody hell! You're going to sell us to the highest bidder?" I accused.

Ever jumped out of her chair and I grabbed her hand before she could do anything stupid. I knew she had a violent streak. I had seen it when she came for me and she had told me she had killed before.

"It's not personal. Please understand. An opportunity came and is giving us the chance to better our lives. Wouldn't you take it?" Mellie asked, leader to leader.

My body was shaking in anger. There were so many things I wanted to say to them, but it was no use. I could tell they would not consider anything I said.

"They have two moons to decide," Mellie said.

"And what then?"

"You go to the one who offers the most."

"Will you allow me to talk to Valinor?" I could not let Ever fall into either Caspar or the Authority's hands. She had to come with me.

She gave a slight nod. "They requested proof of life anyway."

She opened her arm gesturing to the door. We both started to follow her, but she turned back and said, "No. Just you, Empress."

I opened my mouth to protest, but before I could say anything, Ever put her finger on my lips. "I'll be fine," she promised.

Leaning close, I whispered, "Don't try anything."

I was led to a room with one big screen. It must be their control room and they weren't lying when they said they didn't have a lot. It was bare bones. Older communication equipment. Only a few people keeping an eye on things. Nero was in a cage on a shelf. He chittered loud when he saw me.

"Get Valinor on screen," Mellie ordered.

A minute later, Galton and Bristow appeared on the big screen. They both seemed relieved to see me. "Empress! You're alive," Galton spoke.

"Yes."

"Are you okay?"

"I am. I've heard about this ridiculous ransom these people are requesting. Caspar wants me, too."

"I know. Don't worry—"

"Listen. I need you to offer the most, not just for me, but for Everleigh too."

His forehead crinkled. "You're talking about the one who turned you over to Caspar?"

"Yes."

"Empress—"

"That's an order, Galton."

"I think that's enough," Mellie interrupted. "You have your proof of life. Two moons." The screen went dark.

"What will you do with us until then?"

"I can't let you leave, but I won't make you suffer." She turned to her guards. "Take her to a room. Make her comfortable. Keep an eye on her."

"What about Everleigh?"

"She's a criminal. We've taken her to the prison quarters." Mellie waved it off, like she could care less what happened to Ever.

"No. She stays with me."

With lips pinched tight, she said, "Maybe you didn't hear me correctly. She is a criminal."

"I don't care."

"We're not letting her stay in a suite."

"Then put me where you're putting her."

Her hazel eyes bore into me as I challenged her. "Fine. Take her to the prison quarters."

The guard took me by the elbow and escorted me downstairs. He pushed numbers on a keypad and a door opened. Ever was sitting on the floor against the wall with her legs out in front of her and cradling her hand. Both cots had been flipped over and a cup lay in a puddle on the floor in the corner.

Our eyes met and a sad smile touched her lips while one of her shoulders shrugged.

As I crossed the small room, the door banged shut behind me. I dropped down next to her and took her hand in mine. Examining the swollen knuckles, I asked, "Are you okay?"

"I keep thinking this can't get any worse and yet, it continues to."

We're together. It was a thought. Just a thought. I didn't say it out loud. If we were together, we could deal with this.

We sat and we came up with crazy ideas on how to get out of this predicament. We thought up the stupidest, most insane ways to escape. None of them would actually work, but it was fun dreaming up such ideas with her and it passed the time and relieved some of the anxiety.

They brought us food. It wasn't much, but it was more than we had been eating. Afterward we fixed the cots so we could sleep on them that night.

Mellie graced us with her presence again, calling us to a room to talk about what we experienced since leaving our ship. We left a lot of our adventures out. Just relaying the fight with the beasts and a few bad lightning storms.

"Is there a reason why you don't colonize the rest of the planet?" I asked.

"You've seen the reasons. It's too dangerous. The city is surrounded by water, which is good because the grimelings can't swim. But the city is too small to grow food. In order to live, we had to plant crops outside of the city. We built the tunnels so we could get to the crops, but had to add the minefields as an extra layer of protection."

"Why not just kill them?"

"There are more of them than there are of us."

"But they're not intelligent, you said so yourself. Why not just take them out?"

"We don't have the resources to do that, but now we just might. It's one of the things the reward money will help."

"*Ransom* money. Call it like it is," Ever said.

Mellie's eyes shifted to Ever and she frowned. "You're

wanted for many crimes. I could give you over to the Authority just for the fame it would bring me."

"Then why don't you?"

"I need the money more."

Before a fight broke out, I interjected, "If there's nothing more, could we please go back to our room?"

Mellie nodded and the guards returned us to our cell.

There was no fire to keep us warm that night. I curled up on the cot feeling lonely. Eventually I dozed off into a restless sleep.

My mind and my body battled for control as Caspar burst into the room and pulled out a gun. He shot Ever and then turned to me.

"Don't worry, Empress. I won't kill you. Not yet, anyway."

He grabbed me and pushed my face down in a basin of water. Every time he yanked my head out of the water, I glanced at Ever who was lying still on the floor, eyes open, a bullet hole in her forehead. My body was getting tired. I didn't know how much more I could take. He held my head under longer and I started to see a light in the distance.

"Kaci?"

Hands were on me.

"Wake up."

I bolted upright, gasping for air. I reached out and found Ever by my side. She was alive. I was alive. It was a nightmare.

"Breathe."

"I…I can't…" My heart was pounding in my chest and my throat felt like it was closing.

She knelt in front of me, cupping my face in her hands. "Look in my eyes."

I stared into bright, golden depth of her eyes. They were oddly peaceful.

"Breathe." She took my hand, spread it across her breastbone and inhaled deeply, showing me, helping me. "Do it with me."

I nodded and copied her breathing as best I could. Slowly the erratic beating of my heart calmed down and my breathing followed.

"Do you want to talk about it?"

I shook my head. "I don't want to talk about it. I don't even want to think about it. I want it to get out of my head!" A tear dripped down my face. Ever wiped it away with her thumb.

She climbed in the bed with me and lowered me back down. I ignored the way my stomach bottomed out when she held me. I ignored the way my heart kicked against my chest. I ignored the way her body felt when she settled in and molded it against mine. I closed my eyes and let sleep take over, knowing I was safe in her arms.

At first light, I stirred. I could feel Ever's breath on my neck, sending warm tingles throughout my body. Safe. I could spend forever in this room as long as she was with me. So I stayed there in her arms, dreaming about what a life with her might look like.

Ever grew more and more restless as the day wore on, pacing back and forth against the length of the room. She was like a caged animal. I wondered how much of that was built in from the jaguar DNA.

The light in the room dimmed. It would be night soon. The second moon. Ever's pace quickened.

"Can you calm down?" I asked, rubbing my temples.

"How can you just sit there?" she shouted back.

"I can't control what happens today. I'm trying to enjoy the time with you, but..." I stood up and closed the space between us. Her eyes went wide as I walked her back against the wall. "You're driving me crazy."

There it was again, that feeling in my stomach. It wasn't easy to ignore this time. Once more, the air was thick between us. My eyes darted from her eyes to her lips. How I wanted to feel them on mine again. Inching closer, I breathed in deeply smelling her sweet, earthy scent.

I kissed her softly at first, waiting for her to respond. She released a shaky breath, but seemed to relax and smiled against my lips. She opened up, letting me in. Our mouths collided in a wet, passionate kiss. But just as we were settling in for a deep, long, slow kissing, that could potentially last hours, two guards barged in.

"Follow," the one nearest us grunted.

I pulled back, breathing heavily, annoyed that we had been interrupted. After sharing a look with Ever, I pressed my lips to hers one more time and then turned to the guards. My heartbeat returned to normal as we followed them. They brought us to the control room, where Mellie stood watching the monitor. "I figured you'd want to be here when the numbers came in."

"How generous," Ever snarled.

Mellie glanced over at her. "I am sorry, for what it's worth. I just have to do what's right for my people."

"What's the plan tonight? Is it a bidding war?" I asked.

"No. Whoever comes in with the highest price first wins."

Ever looked off to the side. Something had caught her attention. Her eyebrows were furrowed like she was trying to figure something out. As soon as Mellie turned her attention back to the computer, I made eye contact with Ever, asking her what was up. Thankfully she knew what I meant and her eyes moved to the shelves. The jump device was there along with our weapons and in a cage was Nero.

I scooted closer to Ever.

"The jump device. It's on," she whispered.

I shrugged my shoulders to show her I wasn't sure what she was trying to get at.

Her eyes met mine. She used short sentences. "My ship. In range. To jump."

My eyes widened and I nodded.

She hesitated, and said one word, "Risky."

I thought about what Galton had said. While Valinor had plenty of riches, I wasn't sure if we had as much as Caspar or if Galton would do as I asked. There was a chance that Valinor could beat what Caspar would offer, but no guarantee. And Ever, the Authority might want her, but they didn't have the money to pay for her. Which would mean we'd both go to Caspar. Thinking of us both being tortured by him made me sick to my stomach. This could be our way out. Our only option. Definitely worth the risk.

I nodded again.

Her eyes darted back and forth. I knew she was thinking up a plan. We had to get the jump device. She had to at least. There was still a chance Galton would be the higher bid for me.

Seconds later, Ever spun around and disarmed the guard behind her. "Duck!" she yelled and I did.

Using the guard's weapon, she put a bullet in the other

guard's shoulder. Keeping the gun pointed at a very surprised room, she ran over and grabbed the jump device.

I chased after her to the cage that held Nero. I couldn't leave him behind. "What are you doing?" Ever asked as I opened the cage and let Nero climb on my shoulder.

Ever flipped open the device. "It might not be my crew."

"We have to chance it."

Just then the door flew open and more guards poured in. "Drop the weapon!"

Ever aimed the gun, but didn't fire. "We're leaving."

"Take her out!" Mellie ordered.

The guard in front took aim and fired.

"No!" I yelled and jumped in front of Ever. My chest exploded in pain and I stumbled backward into her.

"Kaci!" Ever's arm encircled my waist and she hit the jump button, transporting us to her ship.

"Ever!" a familiar voice shouted. "Oh, shit! What happened?"

Between gasping for air, I looked around at the familiar bridge of the Nirvana and said, "You're home."

I stared into Ever's golden eyes. She had made it back to her ship and her crew was there. They would take care of her. I closed my eyes knowing she was safe. I could go now. In her arms.

CHAPTER SIXTEEN

EVERLEIGH

"No. No. No." My heart pounded violently as I watched Kaci's blue eyes close. "Kaci. Kaci, wake up. You do not get to do this." Looking up at Huxley, Zabe, and Briar, I begged, "Help me."

Despite not seeing them for weeks, and not knowing what was going on, none of them hesitated. They jumped into action like the family they were.

"I'll get us far from this planet. You guys take care of her," Zabe said.

I scooped Kaci up and ran to the medical bay with Huxley and Briar right behind me. Carefully, I placed her on the table and pushed the button to scan her. Nero jumped off and Briar gave a quick yelp then she laughed.

"Hey, little guy," she cooed.

"Briar! Kaci needs help. Nero can wait." I ripped open Kaci's shirt. Blood was pouring out of the gunshot wound in her chest. The scan showed the bullet was close to her heart, but hadn't nicked it. I pushed down on the wound with my hands. Tears poured down my face. "You need to heal. Kaci. Listen to me. You need to heal. I need you."

The monitors started beeping. "She's crashing, Ever," Huxley said.

"Briar, get the shock stick." I wiped my eyes with the back of my blood-covered hands. "Shock her."

Briar put the stick directly above her heart and hit the button sending a current through her body. She jerked, but the monitors didn't stop screaming.

"I need to get the bullet out." I grabbed a pair of forceps. My hand shook so violently that I wasn't sure if I could do it.

Huxley put his hand over my shaking one. "You can do this."

Swallowing back bile, I proceeded to push the forceps into her wound and fish around until I found the bullet. I yanked it out and let it fall to the floor. "Shock her again," I said as I looked around for a cloth. Briar shocked her and I immediately put the cloth over the wound and put pressure on it. The machines settled down. "I need to close the wound."

Huxley got the laser wand out of one of the drawers and handed it to me. Placing the tip onto her wound, I moved it around until it was sealed.

It wasn't pretty, but it didn't have to be. It just had to be closed enough for her to heal. I wondered if there was anything she couldn't heal from. Could she come back from this? What would be too much for her nanites to handle?

When I was finished, I stood next to her, staring, willing her to open her eyes. She had jumped in front of me, saved me, taken a bullet for me. Tears slid down my cheeks. Silent ones at first, but before long the sobbing came.

Huxley put his hand on my shoulder. "Ever. Wash up. It's okay. You can take a minute. She's stable."

I walked over to the sink and scrubbed my hands clean, then I splashed water on my face.

"Are you ready to talk?"

"No. Water?"

"Of course." Huxley strode over to the fridge, got a bottle of water, and handed it to me.

I didn't take my eyes off of Akacia. I watched as her chest rose and fell. Grabbing a chair, I pulled it over to her bedside and sat down, taking her hand in mine.

Zabe walked in. "How is she?"

"Alive," Briar answered.

"How are you?" Zabe directed his question to me.

For the first time since we jumped, I took a deep breath and appreciated where we were. I looked at each of them. "Thank you."

They all smiled, but it was Huxley that said, "You're welcome."

"How did you know?" I asked.

"That little device paid off. I attached it to their comms line. We overheard the call Terronda made to Caspar."

"Nice."

"A ransom, huh? They were going to give you guys to the highest buyer." Zabe bent over and studied Nero.

"I know. Would have been Caspar if it hadn't been for you guys. Tell me what happened after I went to get Kaci." My eyes traveled around the room, stopping at each of them. All three looked like they hadn't slept in weeks, but they didn't look harmed.

"The second we saw him open fire on the Artemis, we fired on him, disabling his ship. He hasn't been able to go anywhere and his comms were down until two nights ago. We stayed out of reach of his weapons trying to figure out what to do. We contacted Valinor, but they wouldn't work with us because we turned the Empress over in the first place. So we were on our own. We knew we had to get close enough for the jump device to activate without Caspar detecting us."

"I still can't believe he has an anti-cloaking device. I guess I should. I mean, he's Caspar. Nothing should surprise me." I shook my head.

"When that call came in, it was the perfect distraction. He wasn't watching us, he was trying to get the money together. We knew for sure where you'd be. We were able to get close enough. Then we hoped the jump device wasn't damaged and you still had it," Briar said.

"Do you know if Caspar...did he kill our families?" I asked.

"We don't think so, but no way to know for sure. With his comms down, he couldn't make any calls to order anyone to kill them. And he couldn't go anywhere. So we're hoping they're still alive." Huxley ran his hand through his silver hair.

Nero jumped up next to Kaci, turned in a circle a few times, and then settled into a comfortable spot.

"Stupid animal," I said with a sigh, but reached out and petted him anyway.

"So, you two work things out? Can't help but notice you're together," Briar said.

"She hates me for betraying her. Not that I blame her. I've been trying to be patient, hoping she'll come around, and I think...she might be. I don't know if she can ever really forgive me and..."

"How did she get shot?" Briar asked.

"She saved me."

"Sounds like she's forgiven you."

I ran my thumb over her knuckles. I didn't answer. I didn't know how to answer. I wasn't sure how long it would take her to heal. Standing up, I peeked under the bandage. The wound was still there, raw and nasty looking.

I turned back around, opened my arms, and my family walked into them. Before long I was blubbering like an idiot. I hoped snot wasn't dripping out of my nose. When we finally broke apart, I dabbed my eyes with my shirt.

"I'm so glad you're all okay. I thought Caspar had killed you. I thought you were dead." My voice cracked.

"We're not. Look. We're right here," Huxley stated, grabbing my hands. "We're all okay."

"We worried the same thing had happened to you," Briar said. "But something told us to have hope."

"I missed you guys," I said through my tears.

"Alright," Zabe teased, pulling me into another hug. "Enough crying." He wiped his own eyes. "I'm going to go check things on the bridge."

Plopping back down in the chair, I rested my head on the table Kaci was laying on. Exhausted, I must have drifted off. When I woke, I changed the bandage. It looked much better. Not completely healed, but getting there.

"Whoa. Her injury looks almost completely gone," Briar commented from across the room.

"She heals," I said.

"What?"

"She has nanites in her. They heal her physical wounds."

"No shit," Huxley said, looking quite impressed.

"Seriously?" Briar's eyes were wide with amazement. "Nanites?"

Zabe stood in the doorway. "Is she safe?"

"What is that supposed to mean?" I asked.

"Does she have nanites in her brain? Could they control her?" Zabe asked.

I hadn't thought of that. "I don't know."

"Depends what kind they are or how they're programmed," Briar answered. "I could run some tests, but I'd like her permission to do so."

"I'm just not sure why she hasn't regained consciousness yet." It's not like there was an instruction manual for her. Maybe one existed for nanites, but if it did, I didn't have it.

"We'll ask her when she wakes up," Briar said.

"Why don't you go shower?" Huxley suggested.

"I'm not leaving her."

"We would come get you if she wakes."

"No."

"How about food. Have you eaten anything yet?"

"No."

"Will you eat if we bring you some food?" Briar's quieter voice asked.

Part of me didn't want to. I wanted to wait for her to wake up and we could eat together. But my stomach rumbled at the mention of food and suddenly I was starving. "Yes."

Nero ate while I ate, then he went right back to resting next to Kaci. He was very much her pet. I hoped he'd be a good friend to her.

As the hours passed, I began to grow more and more anxious. I stared at her, reliving the day's events until I saw her eyes flutter. I waited, but said nothing. She took a deep breath and her eyes opened, searched the room, and landed on me.

The corners of her lips curled in a smile. "Ever." Her voice was hoarse.

"What the hell did you do that for?" I demanded.

"I'll heal. You won't."

"You won't heal if you're dead."

"I'm not dead."

I choked back tears and nodded. The relief I felt now that she was awake and I knew she'd be okay was overwhelming. My heart swelled and I wanted to tell her everything I was feeling, but I was scared. Scared! Me. I was scared of opening up and letting her in. I was afraid that she would reject me, that she'd always see me as someone who betrayed her, or that she didn't feel the same way. I was scared for her, too. My life wasn't a good one. Not in the way she deserved. She deserved more. I was a criminal. Wanted by the Authority. She was an Empress.

It could never be. *We* could never be.

I swallowed hard, shoving the emotions back down. "Briar wanted to know if she could draw some of your blood and run some tests."

"Why? The nanites?" Concern flickered in her eyes.

I nodded, unsure of how she'd feel about it.

"Okay," she agreed, sitting up, and dangling her legs over the side of the bed.

"Zia, call the bridge."

Briar answered, "How is she?"

"Awake and she'll let you run the tests."

"I'll be right there."

"What's going through your mind?" I asked her as we waited.

She chewed on her lip and ran her fingers over the tattoo on her wrist. "If your friends think I'm a freak…"

"I doubt that is what they think of you."

"Hey," Briar said, walking in. "Good to see you, Akacia. Are you sure you're okay with this?"

"Yes." She held out her arm. "I wouldn't mind some answers."

Briar took a small device out of a drawer, pushed Kaci's shirt out of the way, and placed it on her arm. The device drew her blood and collected it in a small vile. "Done," she said. "I'll start the tests."

"Hungry?" I asked Kaci.

"Yeah." Looking down, she peeked under the bandage, and then took it off. There was just a small circle-shaped scar left. It would probably be gone in a few hours. "You ripped my shirt."

"Yeah." I stood up and grabbed the one Briar had brought in earlier. "Here," I said, handing it to her.

She looked right into my eyes as she took off her shirt and put on the other one. Standing up, she took a few steps to the door. Looking back, she said, "Are we going to eat or...?"

Nodding, I stood and walked with her to the kitchen.

I dug out everything I could find. Neither of us spoke while we practically inhaled the food. Kaci sat back in her seat and placed her hand on her belly.

"That was the best meal I've ever had."

"It was hardly anything to brag about. We're just hungry."

"Do you think I could take a shower?"

My cheeks flushed as I thought about her in the shower. "Of course. I can take you to the room you stayed in before."

When the door opened, Nero ran in. Akacia stopped after she stepped over the threshold. Her back still to me, she said, "You could shower with me."

I was sure the blush in my cheeks deepened. I wanted to.

Oh, how I wanted to. But I couldn't. I couldn't tease her or myself that way when I knew that this was destined to end.

"I can't," I said, without further explanation. It took everything in me to turn around and walk away.

Back in my room, I took my own shower, thinking about Kaci the whole time. Dressed in clean clothes, I made my way to the bridge. Huxley had his feet up. Zabe was fiddling with controls. And Briar was looking at maps. They all looked clean and more rested than earlier.

I smiled. I was home.

"Hey, Ever." Briar crossed the room and wrapped her arms around me. "You smell much better."

I let out a laugh. "So glad soap was invented. Kaci?"

"Not yet."

I gave a quick nod. "So where are we? What are we doing?"

"We're here," Briar responded, pointing at a spot on the map. "As far as what we're doing, now that you're back, you can tell us. Are we bringing Kaci home?"

"Yes. How far are we from Valinor?"

"Two nights."

"What about killing Caspar?" Kaci asked from behind.

"Killing him?" Huxley looked between her and me.

"It was something we talked about. That neither of us would be free of him until he's dead. I was sure that he had killed all of you," I explained.

"He would have, but we damaged his ship."

"I assume that even if I offered to buy you all from him, he'd refuse," Kaci said. Nero jumped off her shoulder and onto the table, picking up and looking at the different things lying there.

"He'd never sell us. We're too important to him," Zabe replied.

"So how do we do it? How do we kill him?" Kaci inquired.

"You going to get your hands dirty, Empress?" Huxley asked with a raised brow.

All innocence left her face. "After what he did to me, I'd readily dirty them to end his life."

CHAPTER SEVENTEEN

AKACIA

THE SMILE ON HUXLEY'S FACE disappeared. "I'm sorry. I didn't think."

"It's okay," I replied. My mind started to wander back to Caspar's spacecraft, back to being beaten, back to having my head shoved under water. I could feel the panic rising in my chest, but I took deep breaths and said, "I want him dead. And I'd like to be the one who does it."

"We'd all like him dead," Zabe said.

"You're all under Caspar's thumb, right? Because you're Splicers?"

"You told her?" Huxley shot Ever a look.

"She didn't tell me details. She said that was something you'd have to tell me," I said so they didn't think she outed them.

"Her father was the head of DRI," Ever added.

All three of them looked at me. I shrugged. I knew they knew about me and I wanted them to know I didn't care what they were. "So you guys have animal DNA and I have nanites. We make quite a team."

"You're a keeper, Kaci," Briar said. "A girl who doesn't care what we are and has some secrets of her own."

"I didn't know about any of this prior to Caspar taking me. He thinks I know where my father's research is, which is why he'll keep coming after me."

"And we'll never be safe."

"Do you know about your families?" I asked. "Ever was worried Caspar would kill them all because she rescued me."

"No. We can't exactly ask him," Zabe commented.

"And we don't know where they are so we can't check for ourselves," Briar added.

"How do you know he still has them?"

Briar tapped on the screen in front of her and pictures filled the screen. Pictures of thin people with sad or angry looks in their eyes. "Caspar sent us pictures proving that they were alive, being taken care of, whatever."

"He'd prove food was delivered, but he'd also show us when things went wrong. We'd get pictures of those who had been beaten if we were even late with a delivery," Huxley shared.

"And you can't tell where he has them?"

Briar shook her head. "I've been trying to figure it out. The only thing I could tell was that they were on a planet."

"So we need to take down one evil overlord and find a bunch of Splicers that have been put somewhere in the universe." I looked out the window at the stars. "I need to contact Valinor."

"Of course," Ever responded. "Zia, hail them."

"Hailing Valinor," Zia's voice replied.

A few seconds later, Galton, Vika and Bristow appeared on the screen. Galton scowled. "We told you the last time you contacted us, we wanted nothing to do with you."

I stepped into view. Upon seeing me, Bristow exclaimed, "Kaci! Are you okay? How did you get there? What's going on?"

Before I could answer his questions, Galton's expression softened. "Empress!"

"I'm fine. How are you both? How's Valinor?"

"We're fine. Valinor is fine," Bristow replied.

"You're aboard the Nirvana?" Galton asked.

"Yes."

"Are you safe?"

I kept my hands by my sides. "Yes, Galton—"

Anger flashed in his eyes. "Empress, these people betrayed you before. They'll do it again."

"They also rescued me when they didn't have to. I trust them. I'm safe."

His lips flattened into a thin grim line. It'd been awhile since I'd seen that expression. I was almost happy to see it.

"Very well. Can we send someone for you?"

"No. I have to do something first. Then I'll be home. Are there any issues I need to know about?"

Vika cleared her throat. "Not anything major."

That made me happy. Valinor was safe. "You know what Caspar wanted?" I asked.

"Yes."

"Are we in possession of it?"

"No. It was all destroyed," Galton replied.

I wondered if he was telling the truth, but I had no reason not to trust him. "Watch out for anything odd."

"Meaning?"

"I'm afraid Caspar will retaliate."

Vika looked at the monitors and said, "We'll double security. Keep our eyes on the sky."

Once the call ended, I turned to the crew of the Nirvana. "Let's go get the son of a bitch."

They all laughed. "We need a plan first, Empress," Zabe said, leading us to the table we had played cards on that day that seemed like forever ago. Nero was sitting on the table playing with dice from a game.

"You guys are serious?" Huxley's green eyes searched ours.

Ever and I nodded. I took a deep breath and traced the tattoo on my arm. I didn't look up as I spoke. I couldn't. I was ashamed. "His men attacked me, starved me, and beat me with a chain. Just because I can heal doesn't mean it didn't hurt. Then I was starved and my head held under water until I almost passed out. He needs to die. We'll never be safe. Never..." my voice cracked.

Finally glancing up, I noticed they all had tears in their eyes. Ever's were dripping off of her chin. I grabbed her hand.

"Akacia, we're sorry—"

I wasn't sure I could handle a bunch of apologies, so I held up my free hand. "I know. I understand why. It took some time to get to this point. I don't want to think about what I went through anymore. I want to make the plan to kill him."

"Okay then. Let's talk plans."

"Is his ship his base of operations?" I asked.

"Yes. He doesn't have a planet of his own," Ever answered.

"So we attack his ship. Kill him and destroy all the information and research he has on Splicers and nanites. We can't risk anyone else getting it. We can't let him do to others what he's done to us," Ever said.

"What's the best course of action?"

"We could launch a missile at the ship," Zabe said.

Ever shook her head. "We can't guarantee that everything would be destroyed."

"We could go in ourselves and take him out," Huxley suggested.

"Again that doesn't guarantee that we destroy everything."

"What about a bomb, planted at the core of the ship?" Briar suggested. "The probability that the whole ship explodes is higher using the bomb. To anyone investigating, it'll look like something went wrong with the ship's core. An accident."

Zabe tapped the table. "I agree."

"Zabe, can you make the bomb?" Huxley asked him.

Meeting his eyes, he gave a firm nod. "Absolutely."

They all looked at Ever. "Do it," she said. "How long will it take you to make it?"

"Few days. I need to see if we have everything. Might need to stop by the space station."

"So, who is going to plant it?" Briar asked.

"Me," I said the same time as Ever.

She huffed and rolled her eyes. "Have you ever done something like this before?"

Shaking my head, my eyes drifted to the floor. "But I want him dead. Maybe if I know he's really gone, the nightmares will go away."

The silence was deep. Everybody thought about what it would mean if Caspar were dead.

Zabe spoke first, "I know how you feel, Akacia. Caspar killed my brother in front of me."

My eyes flicked up to his wet brown ones. "I didn't know."

"Of course, you didn't. We all want him dead. Your... experience...has been the most recent. It's fresh. I understand that. Ever is really good at getting in and out of places undetected. It should be her."

Huxley ran his finger over the table. "I don't want her going either. My first instinct is to go to protect her, but I know she is the best person for this job. If it has any chance of working, she has to be the one."

It was late. We had been up talking about the plan until exhaustion finally hit everyone. Ever walked me back to my room.

"I'll...uh...see you in the morning," she stammered then walked away.

I nodded and went in the room. Why didn't I invite her in or give her a goodnight kiss? My heart ached to be with her. I missed her when she wasn't close to me. I missed how the air felt when she was around. I missed how my heart sped up when she looked at me. I missed feeling warm and safe. I wanted to talk to her about what we wanted, but every time I thought about it, I wondered if we defined what we were it would put an end to us.

Someone had left me a T-shirt and shorts to sleep in. After putting them on, I slipped into bed. My body relaxed against the soft mattress, fluffy pillow, and warm blanket. I lay there for a long time staring at the ceiling. This would be the first night Ever and I have been apart since she rescued me. It felt wrong.

Sighing, I turned on my side and closed my eyes.

Later that night, I woke up in a deep sweat and gasping for air. My body trembled even under the blanket. I jammed my eyes closed and fought against the panic. I tried to remember what Ever had taught me, but my brain wouldn't cooperate.

My chest tightened and my throat burned. I pulled at the collar of my shirt. I couldn't do this. Tears streaked down my face. *Ever.* I flew from my room and down the corridor only stopping when I was in front of her door. I pounded on it, hoping she was in there.

The door opened and there Ever stood with a look of concern on her face. "Kaci?" She took a step toward me and pulled me into her arms. "You're safe."

I shook my head, the tears building up so much I couldn't see.

Her arms were around me, holding me close, keeping me safe. "I've got you." She led me inside and to her bed almost tripping over Nero as he rushed in.

CHAPTER EIGHTEEN

EVERLEIGH

K ACI'S ENTIRE BODY SHOOK VIOLENTLY. I took her hand and put it on my chest and I put mine on hers. "Breathe. Slow, deep breaths."

When that didn't work, I remembered what I had read on the computer earlier when I had researched panic attacks. "Focus on what you can see, taste, feel." Her eyes searched the room. "Right here, Kaci. What do you see?"

"You." Her voice was that of a whisper.

"What do you smell?"

"Sweet."

"What do you feel?"

"Your heartbeat."

Finally, her breathing evened out and the panic disappeared from her eyes.

I hated that I could only comfort her. That I couldn't protect her from what was going on in her mind. I loathed that it was because of me she had these attacks.

"Do you want to stay?" I asked.

She nodded.

As much as I wanted to kiss her, I didn't. That wasn't what she needed right now. She needed to be held, to feel safe, loved.

I had wanted to stay with her or invite her to my room when we said goodnight, but I wasn't sure she would want to. I wasn't sure if her feelings would be the same now that we were off the planet.

We scooted up to the head of the bed and I lay down pulling her to me. She rested her head on my chest.

"Plus, your ceiling is much prettier than mine. It means so much more now that I know you're a Splicer."

I laughed and ran my fingers up and down her back tracing her moon tattoos. Now that we were settled, Nero jumped up on the end of the bed, turned in a circle a few times then made himself cozy.

"Does it have to be you?" she whispered.

"Yes." It was a simple an answer. "I am the best one for the job. I have been sneaking in and out of places for a long time. Longer than anyone else on the ship."

"You'll have a bomb in your hand."

"Briar won't turn it on until I'm off the ship. I'll be safe."

"And what if you're not?"

"I will, Kace. I'll come back. Part jaguar, remember?"

"Always land on your feet?" she tried to joke.

"Something like that."

She wiped tears off her cheek. Silence fell around us and we just lay there. Together. Holding on. I could tell the second she fell asleep because her breathing changed. Only then did I close my eyes and let sleep come for me, too.

<hr />

The aroma of eggs wafted down the corridor and my mouth

watered. In the kitchen, I smiled at Huxley. "Smells like heaven!"

"I figured you two would enjoy a good hot breakfast." He grinned and dished out healthy servings of his eggs on waiting plates.

Kaci jumped in a seat and practically inhaled hers. I took my time savoring each bite. Huxley dumped more on her plate. "This is so good. Thank you."

She caught sight of the wolf tattoo on his shoulder. Huxley noticed, too. "I'm spliced with gray wolf DNA, hence the hair," he told her. "I have excellent night vision, run fast, and am loyal."

"And you're a great chef."

He laughed. "Yeah." He looked back at me while she was eating and smiled. I knew what he was thinking. He was impressed this didn't bother her in the least.

Nero jumped up on the table and Huxley placed a piece of egg in front of him. Nero sniffed it, then picked it up with his hands, and stuck it in his mouth. His face scrunched up like he didn't like it, but then he smiled and ran back and forth until Huxley gave him more.

The rest of the crew showed up. "What ever happened to the investigation into Caipra?" I asked.

"The Authority never found the second Wapi spacecraft. The leaders that were killed have been replaced, but some of those replacements have chosen to leave the Alliance."

"A coup?" Kaci asked.

"A failed one. Too many of the new leaders stayed with the Alliance. I'm sure they'll try again," Briar explained. "Tell us what happened on Terronda? What was it like?"

"Horrible," I answered at the same time Kaci said, "Wonderful."

Laughing, she questioned, "Which was it?"

Our eyes locked and I answered, "Both."

We told them about our time on Terronda. I loved watching Kaci tell the stories. She was so animated. I fell a little more in love with her. Soon, I was wrapped up in listening to one of them.

I began to dream a little, thinking of how we could take care of Caspar and find my people. We could cruise around the universe together and have those adventures she always wanted to go on. We would learn everything there was to know about one another. Maybe there could be a happy ending.

Then I thought about the Authority. Even if Caspar was out of the way, we were still fugitives. I couldn't bring Kaci into a life of living on the run. I wouldn't. She deserved normal. She deserved happiness. I couldn't give that to her. I wiped away a tear before anyone had a chance to see it.

***

"I see the way you two look at each other," Briar confronted me when I walked onto the bridge.

We were alone, but I still looked around the room to make sure. I was sure she could see the blood rush to my face. "She's pretty."

"She's beautiful. So are you. But it's more than that."

"I'm attracted to her. That's all."

She huffed and rolled her eyes. "It's so much more than that, Ever. You need to tell her how you feel."

"I can't. She deserves more than a life on the run from Caspar and the Authority."

"You could have other options. You won't know unless you talk to her."

Crossing the room, I went to my control pad. I tapped it a few times and my profile popped up on the screen. It had a picture of me and then a list of things I was wanted for by the Authority. "Theft, destruction of property, assault, murder. This is who I am. Who we all are."

"Not because we want to be."

"Do you think that matters to the Authority? Will they wipe away the charges because we didn't want to be like this?"

"Of course not, but we're not cold-blooded killers. That means something to her. She understands."

"Maybe, but the Authority will always be after us and I can't drag her into a life like that. I have to bring her home and forget about her."

"Just like that? No matter how either of you feels?"

"It's what she deserves."

"I know you think that, but do something for me. Talk to her. Tell her how you feel. See where she stands with all this."

"Fine," I agreed, more to get her to shut up than anything. A small part of me hoped that maybe there was a way and maybe by talking to her we could figure it out.

CHAPTER NINETEEN

AKACIA

BRIAR SPREAD OUT THE MAPS in front of us. "Obviously I can't map out the whole universe. The most I can tell from the pictures I've seen are that the planet can sustain life, but not well. The land looks barren most of the time. I've never seen any indications of water on the planet, but I've only seen so many pictures."

I studied the maps. There were a lot of red Xs on planets. "You've ruled these out?"

"Yes. Ones that are gas planets, unlivable, or we can verify don't look like the pictures."

There were still so many planets without an X. How would they find their people?

"You like Ever," she said.

Startled, I looked up. "I do."

"Have you forgiven her?"

I looked out the window and chewed on my lower lip. "Yes. I understand why she did it, but it doesn't make it hurt any less. I still have nightmares. So, yes, I forgive her, but I still have a lot to work through."

"She's been through a lot with Caspar. He didn't torture

her the same way he did you. She feels responsible for all of us and all the people we left behind. After she turned you over to Caspar, she spent days held up in her room crying and having her own nightmares. She doesn't think we know. She never faltered when we found a way to get to you. I've never known her to have feelings for anyone. Not the kind she has for you."

I wanted to say that I had the same crazy feelings. That I had fallen for Ever the moment I laid eyes on her for the first time back on Valinor. That even though she turned me over, I couldn't hate her, not really. I tried, but deep down...I couldn't. I stayed quiet, unsure if I could trust Briar with my feelings yet. I didn't really trust myself.

"I'd love to see Ever happy. She deserves it."

Looking back down at the maps, I asked, "How many of your people does Caspar have?"

"Originally about a hundred. Not sure how many are left," she answered. "My DNA was spliced with a white tiger."

I looked at her.

"My hair is normally white. I dye it different colors. White is so colorless, ya know?" The corners of her mouth turned up and her blue eyes sparkled.

"I like the pink."

"Thanks."

"Were you all born on a planet?"

"I believe so."

"So suffice to say your families could be on the planet you were born on?"

"It's entirely possible."

"Do you remember anything about living there?"

"No."

"So quick to answer," I said.

"I was young."

"Have you tried hypnosis?"

"No. You think something like that would work if we were so young?"

"I think it's worth trying. One of the space stations might have a hypnotist," I suggested.

"I'll look into it. So it doesn't freak you out that we're part animal?"

"Does it bother you that I'm part robot?"

Briar laughed out loud. "You're not part robot. You just have nanites. Not nearly the same thing."

"And you just have a little animal DNA in you. No biggie."

The rest of the crew came into the room. "So, Zabe says he has almost everything ready," Ever informed us.

Zabe confirmed with a slight nod. "I only need one thing."

"Where do we get it?" Huxley asked.

"The Ignix Station. There's a guy there. I can make a trade."

Concern passed over Ever's face, but she didn't say anything. She just nodded.

Briar's fingers were gliding over the control pad. "We can be there tomorrow." Meeting my eyes, she said, "There's a hypnotist there." Briar filled them in on the rest of my idea and they seemed interested.

"Which one of us will go under hypnosis?" Huxley asked.

"I will," Briar said. "Ever, there's something I want to buy."

Ever's eyebrows arched. "Must be big for you to be asking beforehand."

"I want to buy an AI." Briar bit on her lower lip waiting for Ever's answer.

"You mean a robot?" I asked.

"Essentially, yes. As you know, our computer is very

personable. I'd like to download her into a body. She'd be able to assist us better."

"Very well. If you think you can do that, I'm okay with it."

"Really?" Briar's eyes sparkled.

"Sure," Ever said with a shrug.

Briar threw her arms around Ever and squeezed. "Thank you!"

She sprinted over to the computer and her fingers started flying. Something dinged and she stopped and looked at a different screen. "The results are back on the nanites."

This got everybody's attention.

"Akacia's nanites are specifically healing ones. They are fascinating things. Programmed only to do that one thing."

"Can they heal anything?" Ever asked.

"Not everything. She can still die. Let's say your head gets chopped off—"

"Briar!" Ever barked.

"Sorry. I just wanted you to understand that she can die, and this is only speculation because I have nothing to test my theories on, but if something doesn't kill her instantly, she should heal."

"Can they be reprogrammed?" Huxley questioned.

It seemed like everyone in the room was holding their breath. Briar continued, "Akacia's father was brilliant. I tried to reprogram them, but they can't accept new instructions."

"Could somebody hack them?" Zabe asked.

"They seem to be hack proof, but it's possible something could disrupt them."

"What does that mean?" I inquired.

"I'm still running tests," she answered. "I would have loved to have known your father."

Me too, I thought. I had so many questions and hated that I would never get the answers to them. I sat at the table staring at my veins, running my fingers over them, picturing what the nanites looked like and what they were doing.

———

"Do you want to come to my room tonight?" Ever asked with her eyes on the ground.

Hooking my finger under her chin, I tipped her head up until our eyes met. I smiled and nodded. Words weren't needed. She took my hand and led me to her room. Nero slipped in before the door closed and made himself comfortable at the bottom of the bed.

Ever handed me a pair of shorts and a tank top, which I took and changed right then and there. Her breath hitched when I dropped my pants. I enjoyed watching her blush as her eyes traveled over my almost naked body. Slowly, I put the top on, but I left the shorts on the bed.

After a long moment, she took off her clothes. I bit down on my lip so hard I almost drew blood. She was absolutely gorgeous. I licked my lips. My mouth had suddenly become dry as I gazed at her body. She was everything that I dreamed of. She was my soul mate.

Ever crawled into bed after me wearing only underwear and a camisole, pressing her body to mine. My heart jumped into my throat with her so close to me. Her hand rested on my hip and after a moment, her fingers trailed up my side. A gasp escaped my mouth when she kissed the nape of my neck, my shoulder, and my back. I melted from the inside out.

I turned toward her and our eyes locked. I cupped her face and ran my thumb back and forth across her lips. Quiet moments like these made me happy.

CHAPTER TWENTY

EVERLEIGH

B EING IN BED NEXT TO her was all I ever needed. If I died right now, I'd die happy. Kaci ran her fingers over my back, making shapes, and designs. Suddenly I realized what she was doodling. She was tracing 'I' then a heart then 'U' over and over. My breath caught and my eyes pricked. I swallowed against the ball of emotions in my throat.

I woke up the next morning with her arms around me and her breath on my neck. Our legs were tangled under the sheet. I smiled and closed my eyes again, not wanting to move. She stirred and let out a soft moan. Her lips brushed against my neck and trailed from my ear down my shoulder and up again, kissing, sucking, nibbling on my ear. I remembered what she was tracing on my back before falling asleep.

"Oh, Kaci…" I mumbled, trying to turn around, but she stopped me.

"Morning breath," she giggled, covering her mouth.

I used the bathroom first. Something caught my attention in the mirror. Getting closer, I ran my finger over the small, purple bruise on my neck. With a smirk on my face, I turned around and looked at her. She was propped up on the bed watching me.

"You marked me," I said.

She laughed. "I did."

I crossed the room in two strides and put my mouth on her neck. "I should mark you."

She laughed. "It wouldn't stay. I'd heal."

"Let's find out." I began kissing and sucking on her neck until a pink spot appeared. I don't know why, but it turned me on to see my mark on her neck. Before my lips reached hers, she said, "Nope. My turn for the bathroom."

Practically skipping over to my dresser, I opened it and my eyes rested on her ring. I had forgotten about it. I picked it up and waited for her to come out of the bathroom. I held it up as soon as she did.

"My ring!"

"I found it after you...left."

"I wasn't sure if I had it while on Caspar's ship. My memories are a little fuzzy. I'm so glad I didn't lose it."

As I slipped the ring back on her finger, I felt the heat rise to my cheeks. Kaci was blushing too as she stared at our hands. Before she could say anything else, I reached back in the drawer and grabbed a clean outfit. She laughed.

"What?"

She looked through my clothes. "You seriously don't have anything other than black."

"Not really."

She huffed and put the clothes on. "They're a little tight."

"You have more curves than I do." I placed my hands on her hips.

"Are you calling me fat?"

Laughing, I said, "No way. Just more curves and I like them. I like them a lot."

She threw her head back and laughed. The sound was so beautiful it left me wide-eyed. When she settled, I captured her lips. I tightened my grip on her hips, silently wanting more. She moaned loudly as our lips moved together. The kiss was soft and tender, hard and rough, slow and meaningful, fast and frenzied and I loved every second of it.

Her hands were at the back of my neck, tangled in my hair. I knew she wasn't sure what was next and either was I. I didn't think she was ready for me to make love to her, but I didn't want to stop.

My intercom buzzed. I heard it, but my lips didn't respond to my brain telling them to stop. It buzzed again. Kaci smiled against my mouth. "I think someone is trying to get your attention."

"I don't care." I mumbled.

A third buzz made me pull away. I pressed my forehead to hers and tried to catch my breath. Swearing silently, I spun and hit the button to answer the door. Briar stood there. She looked from me to Kaci and down to her feet, and then blushed something awful. "I'm sorry. I didn't realize... We're almost to the space station. You wanted me to let you know."

"Thanks."

"I'm guessing she doesn't normally answer the door in her underwear?" Kaci smiled.

I looked down and realized I was still in my cami and underwear. Heat filled my cheeks.

Briar laughed. "Not usually."

Kaci closed the space between us. In a swift move, she

seized my lips for one last searing kiss and then slipped out the door. "I smell eggs."

Nero took off after her.

Briar tore her eyes away from Kaci walking away. "Well, that was…um…wow! You are so whipped."

Trying and failing to hide my smile, I asked, "How long?"

"You have time to eat, though you should get dressed first."

"I'll be right there."

The door closed and I sat on my bed for a minute reliving everything that had happened since the night before. I needed to talk to Kaci, really talk to her. I knew I shouldn't get my hopes up, but the way she made me feel convinced me it was worth it.

I finished getting dressed and hurried to the kitchen for breakfast. They were all seated at the table eating when I walked in. I helped myself to some eggs and sat down. Zabe and Huxley were talking about the space station. Briar chatted with Kaci. I sat back and watched them all interact. They were comfortable with each other. My crew didn't look at Kaci as an outsider. And she shined here with them.

"You've got something on your neck," Zabe said to me.

Briar spit out her drink while Kaci laughed.

"What?" He studied me and then his eyes widened. "Oh!"

I glanced at Kaci's neck. Sure enough, hers was gone. She caught me looking at her and smiled, causing my heart to beat frantically again. Damn! Never thought that I would find someone who made me feel the way she did.

Back on the bridge, I sat at my control pad, and refreshed my memory of the layout of Ignix Station.

Kaci placed her hands on my shoulders and massaged them. "Tell me."

I let out a sigh. "This station isn't one of the ones I'd rather go to."

"Because of the Authority?"

"Yes."

"So we have to be extra careful."

We. She had nothing to fear from the Authority. Yet she lumped herself right in with us. Just another reminder that she wasn't actually one of us no matter how comfortable she was here.

<hr />

Once we docked, Huxley, Briar, and Zabe disembarked. All of us had to go this time. It made me nervous to leave the ship unprotected, but it couldn't be helped. Zabe went to find the person he was supposed to meet. Huxley went to the casino. Now that Caspar wasn't paying us, we'd need the money. Briar headed to find the hypnotist.

"So what do we need to do?" Kaci asked, walking toward the door.

"I need to get some supplies loaded onto the ship, then meet with somebody. After that, I'm done. You can go do whatever you want. You don't have to—"

"I'm staying with you," she cut me off.

I bit my lip to hide my smile. "Let's go."

Briar had called ahead to make sure Lael would be working. He was the one person at this station I trusted. Not only have we been working with him a long time, but I had enough dirt on him that he'd do anything I asked. He met us at the dock station.

"Everleigh, it's been a while. What do you need?"

"Supplies. All the normal stuff."

"No problem. Shouldn't take long."

I handed him the payment. "How is the Authority's presence?"

"On a scale of one to ten, maybe a four."

I held up a wad of money. "There's a tracker on my ship. It's disabled. I need it removed and left on the ship so we can analyze it."

He arched a brow. "Got it."

Revealing my weapon, I said, "Only your guys go on my ship. No one else."

"Understood."

I stayed to the back corridors, hoping to avoid all security personnel. Kaci followed right behind me. My thoughts went back to the fact that she was hiding in the shadows for me and that wasn't right. She was good, special, everything that I wasn't and everything that I couldn't have. No matter how I felt about her, or how she felt about me, we could never be together.

Pausing outside a door, I said, "You should stay out here."

"Don't push me away."

There was something I had to do and I didn't want her to be involved or even see. "Kaci—"

"Whatever it is, Ever, I can handle it." She planted a quick kiss on my lips.

Taking a deep breath, I knocked on the door. When it opened, a young dark-skinned guy with dreads greeted us.

"Everleigh."

"Hey, Rigby."

His eyes drifted to Kaci. "Come in."

"She's with me."

He nodded and closed the door behind us. "What can I do for you?"

I took a container out of my pocket and held it up. "I'm here to trade."

Rigby nodded and led us to another room where an older man with slick-backed hair sat. "Siarl, you have visitors."

My heart thudded in my chest, not because I was scared of Siarl or his men, but because I didn't like Kaci seeing the criminal side of me. Maybe it was a good thing. Maybe it would scare her off.

"Is that the toxin?" Siarl asked.

"Yes. It will paralyze anyone who breathes it in, kill anyone who is injected with it. No trace. No blood test can detect it."

"Excellent. Our offer stands."

"Actually, I'm going to need more."

Siarl stood, his gray eyes drilling holes into mine, but I held my ground. "I should kill you."

"Then my team will kill *you*." I didn't back down. "Many others want to get their hands on this. Maybe even some of your enemies. I'll walk away. Sell it to someone else."

"You don't want to make an enemy of me, Everleigh." He looked at Kaci and I wrapped my empty hand around my weapon, just in case he tried something.

"I certainly don't, Siarl. This is just business. I need twice what you offered." I shook the container to refocus his attention. "There's plenty here. It'll last a long time."

His lips flattened into a thin line, but then he nodded and took a step backward. "You're playing with fire, Everleigh. You better keep an eye on what you value most." His gaze shifted to Kaci again.

Rigby held out a box and I held out the container. Slowly, we made the trade. Without another word, I led Kaci out of the room. Back in the corridor, I let out a deep breath. With the box tucked under my arm, I took Kaci's hand and led her to a storage company. I went straight to my locker, placed my finger on the pad, and stuck the moneybox inside.

After closing it, I stole a glance at Kaci. She was chewing on her lip and tracing the tattoo on her arm. It was what she did when she was thinking. I wasn't sure whether or not to say something or just pretend she didn't see any of that.

I decided to go with, "Are you okay?"

"What?" She looked up and caught my gaze. "Yeah. I'm fine. No…that's not really truthful. Did you really just sell a toxin that'll kill people?"

"Yes."

"And you're okay with that? Knowing that someone will die because you gave it to that monster?"

"I don't think about it. I can't. I just do it for the money." It wasn't the first time I had felt guilty selling stuff like that, but it was the first time I hadn't wanted to ever do it again. "I'm sorry. I'm a criminal, Kaci. You do know what that means? I do bad, illegal things. It's my way of life."

"It doesn't have to be."

"But it is." Guilt brought tears to my eyes. I wiped them away angrily. "It's who I am."

"No. I do not accept that. You are kind, loving, caring, and wonderful. You're smart and tough. You're sensitive and vulnerable. You're so much more than a criminal. I wish you could see yourself the way I do." She cupped my face and held my gaze.

A tear rolled down my cheek. "So you don't hate me?"

"Of course not." She wiped my tears with her thumbs.

"We can go back to the ship now. Or do something here?"

"What are my choices?"

"Eat, shop, get pampered. What I'd really like to do…"

"Yeah?"

"Take you on a real date, but…"

"We have to keep a low profile."

Looking at the floor, I mumbled, "I'm sorry."

"Don't be sorry." She pulled me to her and pressed her lips to mine for a short, chaste kiss.

"How is this keeping a low profile?" I teased.

"Fine." She huffed. "Let's shop."

We strolled around a clothing shop, looking through the racks. Kaci held up a blue, cold shoulder, flutter top. "Try this on."

Narrowing my eyes, I asked, "Why?"

"Because I asked. Because it's blue and not black."

I took the shirt and her hand and dragged her to the back of the store. The saleslady gave us the evil eye as I pushed her into the dressing room before me. I'm sure she thought we were going to steal something. Kaci leaned against the wall while I changed into the shirt. I could see her in the mirror biting her lip. The shirt was nice, different than anything I've ever worn, but I did feel sexy in it and the blue reminded me of her eyes.

"I like being able to see more of your skin." She took a step forward and ran her hands up my arms all the way to my shoulders. She pressed her lips to the purple mark she had left behind. "I especially like seeing my mark on your skin."

"Wow! I never knew you were so territorial."

A smile spread across her face. "You have lots to learn about me."

I started pulling the shirt off so she couldn't see the expression on my face. The one of pain, of guilt. I needed to get her home where she belonged. I needed to get her safe. She couldn't stay with me, but I couldn't tell her that. Not yet. I blinked to keep the tears away.

"Do you like the shirt?"

"Yeah." I put my own shirt back on.

"I'll buy it for you." At the register, Kaci's face dropped. "I just remembered I don't have any money on me."

The saleslady pursed her lips when I laughed. "Of course not. Don't worry. I'll pay."

CHAPTER TWENTY-ONE

AKACIA

EVERLEIGH WAS HOLDING SOMETHING BACK. I just didn't know what it was and I didn't want to pester her. She'd tell me when she was ready.

As we walked down the corridor, I noticed Ever stiffen. Following her gaze, I saw a couple uniforms walked toward us. They didn't look to be after us, so I took her hand and squeezed it as we kept walking. She let out a sigh of relief when they passed.

At the hostess desk, Ever asked, "Can we sit at the bar?"

The lady nodded and pointed to the back of the room.

We sat on stools and the bartender asked what we wanted. Our drinks arrived quickly along with a bowl of pretzels. We talked while munching and sipping our drinks.

A calm, relaxed feeling came over me. My body felt warm and tingly. I put my hand on Ever's arm and traced her tattoo.

"My crew really likes you," she said.

"I like them, too. They feel like family. Besides Bristow, there's nobody back on Valinor that I really hang out with. It's always learning and leading. There's nobody who wants to be my friend or likes me for me. It's nice to have that. Is it hot in here?"

She grinned. "It's the alcohol."

"Right." I couldn't take my eyes off of her. Glancing at her neck, I could barely make out the hickey in the dim room. I thought about how I'd like to make more marks on her body.

"I have feelings for you," she muttered.

"I gathered from all the kissing."

She shot me a look that told me this was not the time for sarcasm.

"I have feelings for you and I know I can't be with you. It's too dangerous. Between being a criminal and being on the run from the Authority, it's not a life I want you to have."

"Shouldn't I have a say in this?"

"There's no way out. Not one I can think of and I've been doing a lot of thinking. I just wanted you to know."

We sat there in silence for a while. I blinked to keep the tears away. I understood what she was saying, though I didn't agree.

"We have today. That's what matters. Tomorrow's not promised for anyone. So live for today, without hesitation." And with that, I leaned over and kissed her.

"We should go."

Picking up my glass, I swallowed the last bit of my drink. "I'm going to go to the bathroom. Meet you up front?"

She held up her glass, which was still a third of the way full. "Be there in a few minutes."

I was waiting for Ever at the front of the restaurant when I heard, "The crew of the Nirvana." My ears perked up and I took a step closer. "A male in the casino, female here."

"Is she still here?"

"Yes."

I slipped away and back to the bar where Ever was finishing her drink. I leaned down. "You need to come with me now."

She met my eyes and then stood. I led her away from the wall until the Authority passed by. Then I hurried to the side door and pushed her out in front of me. "Is the ship docked under a fake name?"

"Always."

"Good. Go. Get back to the ship. Get ready to go."

"What is going on?"

"They know we're here. I'll get the others."

"Kaci, no. I'm not putting you in danger."

"I'm the only one they're not looking for."

She knew I was right, but I could see the war raging inside her head.

"You have an earpiece, right?"

"Yeah, but they probably have them off." She tapped her ear as we kept walking. "Hux? Zabe? Bri?" She shook her head. "Nothing."

I knew where Huxley and Briar were so I asked, "Where's Zabe?"

"I'll get him," she said. I opened my mouth to argue, but she kept talking, "I know where he is and I know who he's with. It's too dangerous for you to go. You get the others."

I didn't want to let her go. I was scared she'd get caught. "Ever…"

"I'll be okay, Kace." She turned and rushed off. My heart lurched and I chastised myself for not opening up more to her about how I felt. What if I never got another chance?

Looking at a map, I made my way to the casino. I was about to do things I never imagined myself doing. First, I stopped at a wig shop. When the salesperson wasn't looking, I put one on and walked out. I could return the wig when I was done, but right now, I needed a disguise. Not that anyone was looking for me, but so I wouldn't be identified when they went back and looked at the recordings.

Two guards stood at the entrance of the casino. Holding my head high, I walked right past them. I scanned the room as I weaved in and around people and the betting machines. Finally my eyes landed Huxley. I didn't go to him right away. I had to assess the situation first. There were four uniforms watching. I wasn't sure what they were waiting for, but I devised a plan in my head and hoped it would work.

Grabbing a drink off a waiter's tray and downing it— because let's face it, for what I was about to do, I needed the liquid courage—I walked straight to Huxley with a smile on my face. He looked up, surprise written all over his face. I ran my hand through his hair and sat on his lap.

"Are you almost done? I'm getting very impatient." I planted a kiss on his lips and his mouth dropped open. I kissed his neck and then whispered, "The Authority knows you're here. We need to get you out of here and back to the ship. Cash out."

"Oh darlin', I'm ready." He pushed over his chips and the dealer gave him a card, which he handed to me. Standing, he put his arm around me, and I led him toward the biggest group of people I could find. A quick sideways glance and, I saw the guards moving in.

"There's a side exit. Go."

"What about you?"

"I've got this." I almost scared myself on how well my plan was working. He split and I took off the wig and tucked it in my shirt. I walked right up to a booth and handed over the card. They gave me money. More money than I had ever seen.

"Do you have a bag?"

"A bag?"

"Shopping bag?"

"Um…" He looked around and picked something up from the floor. "Here."

It was small, but it would do. "Thanks." I took the bag, shoved the money in and walked out. Nobody was looking my way. I slipped back in the wig shop and replaced it perfectly.

"Do you wish to try on a wig?" a voice surprised me from behind.

"No, thank you." I smiled and hurried out of the store to the hypnotist's office. I stepped up to the counter.

"May I help you?" the lady behind the desk said.

"I'm looking for my…sister. She has pink hair. She said she'd be here."

"I can't give out any information."

I thought for a moment. "Well, can you give her a message from me. Can you tell her that her sister needs to speak with her immediately?"

"But then you'd know if she was here."

"I already know she's here. I'll turn around, so I don't technically see you leave. Go out the door. You can tell her. She won't mind." I placed a coin on her desk.

The lady mashed her lips together and tapped her fingers on the desk. Finally, she reached out and grabbed the coin. "Fine."

I paced the room as I waited wondering if Ever and Huxley made it back okay. After a few long moments, Briar came out with an amused look on her face. "Hey, sorry I was late."

"No problem. Did you get what you needed?"

"Maybe. What's up?"

"Mom needs us."

"Okay, let's go." She turned to the lady behind the desk. "Thank you."

We walked calmly down the corridor. Briar hit her earpiece. "Ever? Yeah. We're on our way. Everyone else? Good." She glanced over at me and said, "Everyone else made it back."

"Hey! You there!" a voice behind us yelled. "Stop!"

"Don't turn around," Briar said. "Keep your head down."

"Authority!" they yelled. "Stop or we'll shoot!"

"There's a store coming up. We can go through it, try to lose them, and get to the ship," Briar said.

We took off running and a tranquilizer dart whizzed past me. Ducking into the store, we weaved through aisles and came out the other side. Briar led me down a dark, back corridor. I could hear shouting, but no more shots were fired. We got to the bay and boarded the spacecraft.

"We're here, Ever. Go," Briar said. Turning to me, she said, "Hang on."

I grabbed ahold of a nearby railing as the ship shot into space and left the station far behind. Briar and I made our way to the bridge. Ever's face relaxed when our eyes met. "You okay?"

"Yeah."

"This girl," Huxley said. "She's incredible."

Heat rushed to my face.

"I'm serious." He grinned.

"I agree," Briar said.

Before they said anything else, I asked, "Zabe, did you get what you needed?"

"Yes. I'm going to go work on it right now."

"Zabe?"

"Shouldn't take long, Ever." He strode out of the room.

She nodded. "We stocked up on supplies—"

"Oh, and I got the money." I tossed the bag on the table. Noticing Briar spreading out her maps, I asked, "Briar, did you learn anything?"

"I think…they may be on one of these planets." Her hand hovered over an area and then another. "Or these."

Huxley and Ever joined her and examined the area she was pointing at.

"What did you remember?"

"You could see two other planets from ours. The sunstar was a blue giant. I don't remember seeing much else, but I did remember some things I overheard. The adults were talking about the harsh winters. Someone said the reason Caspar had left them on such a desolate planet was so they had to depend on him."

"Where is Caspar's ship now?"

"Here." Briar pulled something up on the screen. "Once someone came to them to fix their engine, they went to the station for more repairs. They just left that station. He's heading this way." She pointed. "We can intercept around the time we'd be waking up."

"Sounds like a plan."

"Also, I picked out an AI. She was delivered onto the ship. I'll get her ready when I have a minute," Briar said like setting up an AI was the easiest task in the universe.

CHAPTER TWENTY-TWO

EVERLEIGH

THE DOOR CLOSED BEHIND US and Kaci immediately took my hands. "What's wrong?"

"What happened today…"

"Everyone is okay."

"You were in danger, Kaci."

"All of us were."

"But you don't deserve it."

"That's over. We got away. Let's focus on what we have to do now."

I didn't know if I liked that she brushed it off so easily or if it infuriated me. "It should be a simple in and out."

"You'll come back?" she said.

"I will." I really wasn't the least bit scared. She seemed more than just worried about me. "Is there something else on your mind?"

"I kissed Huxley." Guilt flashed in her eyes.

I held back a chuckle. "You did?"

"To get him out of there. It was just a cover though, I—"

I cut her off mid-sentence with a kiss. She instantly kissed me back. Hungry and deep kisses. My hands found the small of her back and pulled our bodies flush against each other.

"Anything else you want to get off your chest?"

"Just this." She pulled her shirt over her head.

My eyes mapped over her exposed flesh and rested on her beautiful breasts. "Damn." I bit my lip. Unable to control myself, I lunged forward and seized her lips in a heated, feverish rush.

My hands roamed the vast expanse of her back and traced her curves. Her skin was smooth and warm. Pulling away, my eyes locked with her bright blues. I ran my thumb over her swollen, moist lips.

I kissed along the side of her neck, memorizing the smell of her hair and taste of her skin. Pressing her up against the wall, I moved my thigh in between her legs. She gave a low hum of approval and grinded her body against me, which set my body on fire. Her hands went under my arms and her fingernails dug into my back before she pulled me closer. Trailing kisses along her jaw, under her ear, and across her chest, I led her to my bed where I lowered her down.

After a while, we stopped kissing and she curled up in my arms and fell asleep. I held her all night, hardly sleeping. My mind was in overdrive thinking about how we barely escaped the Authority. They weren't someone we could kill to keep them from coming after us. We couldn't pay them off either. To them, we were criminals. It was either stay on the run or be locked up. I knew I should keep my distance, but I couldn't. She smelled like the most perfect day, a dream come true. Happiness. I knew I was being selfish. I just didn't know how to stop.

Morning came too fast. We dressed in silence while Nero chased around this stupid toy Briar had bought him at the space station. I pulled my hair back in a ponytail to keep it out of my way. "Food?"

"Too nervous," Kaci answered.

"You should have something."

"I feel like I'm going to throw up."

"There's really nothing to worry about," I tried to reassure her.

Our eyes met and she nodded, but something made me think she wasn't just worried about me planting the bomb.

"Is there something else going on?" I asked.

"No. I just don't want to lose you."

"You won't." It wasn't a lie. I was hers. I would always be hers. Whether or not I could be with her was another story.

Over the intercom, Briar's voice told us that we were close.

"Go," Kaci said. "I'll be there in a minute."

<hr>

Zabe walked onto the bridge with a sleek silver canister in his hand. "It's finished."

"It's so small," Kaci stated.

"This gorgeous thing will destroy the ship." Carefully, he placed it on the table. "All you have to do is get it to the core of the ship. It's magnetic, so you can attach it to pretty much anything there. Then you get out of there. Briar can set it off remotely as soon as you jump back. We'll then have thirty seconds to hightail it out of the way."

"Let's do this." I picked up the device.

"They will be able to detect us. We won't stay stationary, we'll have to randomly move around, but we'll stay in jump range," Huxley said.

"Almost through his security," Briar reported. "Caspar upgraded since the last time we hacked in, but I've got this."

I didn't want to say anything to Kaci. I knew if I did, she'd worry more, but I didn't want to go without a single word just in case something did happen. Apparently she felt the same way because she closed the space between us and planted her lips on mine for a long minute. It wasn't a passionate or gentle kiss, but it was one that left my lips wanting more.

Glancing at Huxley, I said, "Keep your hands off my girl."

He let out a loud laugh and Kaci turned bright pink, while the other two looked confused.

I stepped into the jump circle, keeping my eyes on her, and when Briar gave the okay, I pushed the button. Suddenly I was in the core of Caspar's ship.

With no time to waste, I wove in between the machinery and placed the device right on the central computer. Just like Zabe said, it stayed there. Easy. With a nod of satisfaction, I placed my finger on the jump device, but before I could press the button, a voice came through my earpiece, "Ever?"

"Yeah, Briar?" I whispered.

"Akacia took the other jump device. There's a gun missing, too."

"Fuck." What was she thinking? That was a stupid question. I knew exactly what she was thinking. Revenge. Personal revenge. She wanted to be the one to actually kill him.

This was what she was holding back.

I should have seen it coming.

"Can you tell where she is?" I asked, desperate.

"Not for sure. My guess is she's going for the bridge."

"I'm going after her."

"Be careful, Ever," Briar said.

Seconds later, I heard gunshots.

CHAPTER TWENTY-THREE

AKACIA

I LANDED IN AN UNKNOWN ROOM. Nobody had taught me how to use the jump device, so I had to guess at some of the settings. I had to find Caspar and fast. I wanted to be the last face he saw before he died.

As I rushed through the corridor, I passed a room with large windows that looked to be a lab. I stopped and after making sure nobody was inside, I entered.

One wall of the room was lined with large cages, about ten of them. I saw a flash of movement in the last cage. I crept closer and saw a human-shaped figure.

A low growl appeared to come from him. Curiosity got the best of me and I took a few more steps toward it. The closer I got, the more I realized this creature wasn't human. Fur sprouted in patches all over his body. One of his hands looked normal and human, while the other was a paw.

Suddenly, he let out a loud growl and started banging on the cage. Drool dripped from his sharp, canine-like teeth. Looking in his tortured filled eyes, I had no doubt that this was an experiment gone wrong.

I backed away from the feral creature in the cage. Once I

was far enough away, the creature calmed back down. I turned to the computer.

After a few keystrokes, I was searching through Caspar's files, trying to find out what he knew. My heart picked up its pace when I saw one labeled Splicers. Opening it, I found pictures of people that I could only assume were Splicers in cages. Looking back at the metal boxes, at the creature in the corner, something clicked and my stomach churned. I realized the reason Ever reacted in the tunnel on Terronda the way she did had to be because she was kept in one of these cages at some point. I couldn't tell if she was one of the ones pictured, but it made sense.

Rage filled me. I picked up the heaviest thing I could find and pounded the screen, cracking it. Of course that wouldn't do anything—the files were stored in a central computer—but it felt good. The bomb would take care of the files.

It took a ridiculous amount of time to find the bridge. I thought for sure I was going to die in the explosion, but I couldn't go back. Caspar was on the bridge with one of the guards that tortured me.

"It's definitely the Nirvana, but they keep moving. They know we can see them," the guard said.

Caspar sighed like he was annoyed. "Should have killed them when I had the chance. As soon as you can, fire on them. Once their ship has been destroyed, I want to fill the cages with Splicers, kill the rest, and personally go to Valinor. I will get what I want."

"Like bloody hell you will," I said, stepping into the room with my weapon drawn.

After Caspar's initial shock, a sly smile spread across his face. "Empress. Miss your time here?"

Everything around me faded away. Caspar's smile reminded me of how he looked at me when he or his men were torturing me. In my mind, I saw the chain being swung around in his hand. The basin of water. The chair I had sat in while being beaten. The cages where they kept Splicers. My hand trembled, but I kept it pointed at him.

"Have you ever used one of those before?"

I tightened my grip. What was I waiting for? Why didn't I just shoot him?

"You pull that trigger and you make yourself a criminal. You will always be looking over your shoulder. Maybe that's what you want. You know you're a freak now."

Fury poured through my veins and I pulled the trigger. First at Caspar, then at the guard when he went for his gun. They both went down, someone shouted, an alarm rang out and I could only stand there and watch the blood pool around their bodies.

Ever burst into the room with eyes wide and searching. When they landed on me, her face relaxed. She looked past me to Caspar and the guard.

Loud yells came from down the hallway. Ever took my hand and in seconds we were back on the Nirvana.

"Give me the gun," Ever's voice sounded far away. "Kaci… you're safe."

My hands trembled but I couldn't seem to let go of the gun.

"Maybe it's best if you guys leave now."

"We're not leaving, Ever."

"You don't have a choice. I'm ordering you to!" she yelled.

Huxley opened his mouth.

"Now!"

Nobody moved. Ever let out an exasperated sigh and turned back to me. "Kaci? Can you hear me?"

I could, but it felt like I was under water and she was calling to me from the surface. My chest started to constrict. Everything seemed to be moving in slow motion.

"Kaci." She put her hands on mine. "I'm going to take the gun, okay?"

My grip tightened.

"You're safe. Breathe. Nobody here will hurt you. Please, Kace, come back to me." She positioned herself right in front of me.

I blinked a few times forcing myself to hear her words. I let her take the gun. She placed it in her waistband and then wrapped her arms around me.

"Now, Briar!"

There was a bright light and the Nirvana lurched just before kicking into FTL speed.

Ever cupped my face and covered it with kisses. "Why did you do that? He would have died in the blast. You didn't have to kill him."

Caspar was right. I had blood on my hands now.

Not letting go of my hand, Ever closed the space between her and Huxley. She whispered to him and he nodded.

"Come on," Ever led me away from the bridge and back to her room. She turned on the shower. "Take a hot shower."

I didn't move. Instead I stared at the floor.

"Hey," she said, her thumbs wiping away my tears. "If you don't take off your clothes, I'll take them off for you and believe me I do not want the first time I strip you down to be remembered this way."

My hands moved and my clothes fell to the floor. I stepped

into the shower. The hot water mixed with my tears as it flowed over my body until I finally collapsed onto the shower floor and pulled my knees to my chest.

After a while, I forced myself to get out and dried off. Ever had left me some clean clothes in the room, so I got dressed. I sat on her bed staring off into space. Silently, she knelt behind me and started braiding my hair, which felt heavenly. When she finished, she sat beside me. I put my head on her shoulder and she took my hand.

"Sorry about earlier," I mumbled.

"I know."

"I froze. I just..."

"I know."

We stayed there for I don't know how long, until Ever decided I had to eat. She dragged me to the kitchen and put a bowl of soup and some bread down in front of me. I took a few bites before pushing the rest of it around with my spoon.

"Isn't it good?"

"Yeah. Just not hungry."

"I know you just did something you never thought you'd do—"

"I just killed. Became a murderer. Yeah, so, I'm not hungry."

Ever looked away. "Okay. We'll come back when you do get hungry. Briar's waiting for us. We have to make a decision."

When we reached the bridge, the rest of the crew was there.

"I'm sorry," I said to them all.

"Nothing to be sorry for," Zabe said, surprising me.

"He's right," Huxley said. "It's happened to all of us."

"Now what?" Briar stood at the controls ready to plug in coordinates.

I turned to Ever. "I need to go back to Valinor."

"I understand."

"I need answers." I looked at her and everyone else faded away. "Will you come?"

"To Valinor?"

"I don't want to do it alone."

"Yeah. Will they let me?"

Smirking, I answered, "I think you're forgetting who the Empress is."

Laughing out loud, she said, "Okay. If you promise they won't kill me on sight."

"I'll just jump in front of you."

All color drained from her face. "Don't do that again."

"So?" Briar said, reminding us she was there. "To Valinor?"

Ever nodded, though I noticed the look on her face wasn't one of happiness.

I retreated back into my head again while they talked. My finger found the tattoo on my arm and ran over it again and again.

"We need to find our families soon," Briar said softly. "We have no idea how long they'll survive without Caspar."

"We will. We just need to get her home first." I heard Ever say. "I'm going to get her to bed."

"I'll stay here and monitor the comms for news about Caspar's ship," Briar said.

Zabe and Huxley were playing an intense game of Loaded when Ever took my hand and led me to her room.

I didn't sleep that night. Ever sat up against the head of her bed with my head in her lap. For a long time, she was quiet, then she said, "We were on a mission for Caspar. He wanted this antique from the Mezzi Corporation. Briar and I went in for it. We were caught. A guard pushed Briar into me, knocking me over. Before I could get up, he was on top of me and pinning me down. The knife in his hand was coming at me. Briar jumped on his back and stabbed his shoulder. He dropped the knife in his hand, grabbed her and threw her into a wall, knocking her out. It gave me just enough time to get the dagger I had hidden in my boot. When he reached for his knife, I swung mine, slicing his throat. Then, like that wasn't going to kill him, I took it a step further and thrust the knife into his heart. He fell onto me, covering me in his blood. I pushed him off, scooped up Briar and the antique, and jumped out of there."

I was quiet while picturing the scenario. "That's different," I said softly. "You were protecting Briar, defending yourself. You're not a cold-blooded killer."

"Either are you."

I nodded, but her words meant nothing.

The next day, I surrounded myself with the crew and Nero; staying busy, talking, playing card games, petting Nero. Anything to keep from thinking of what I had done. A few times, I found myself at the window just staring out into space. So much out there to explore.

One time, I turned around and Briar had the maps out again. Walking over, I asked, "Are you still trying to decide where to go first?"

"Yeah. There are a few different blue giants with planets close together."

"Go to the closest one first?" I suggested.

"That's the logical thing to do."

"Makes sense to me."

She nodded and pulled me into a hug. "I'm going to miss you."

"Me too." My voice quaked.

Ever and I even went to the weapons room to spar. I had forgotten just how impressive the room was. Spending time with Everleigh, Huxley, Zabe, and Briar had made me see them as less threatening than they actually were. I had allowed the fact that they were criminals to slip my mind. This room brought all of that back. They were all lethal.

"You should try the punching bag," she suggested, holding up the tape to wrap my hands. "It helps me with my anger."

I glanced over at the bag hanging from the ceiling. "Really?"

"Don't knock it 'til you try it." She positioned herself behind the bag. "C'mon."

I taped up my hands and then threw a punch.

"Harder." Her golden eyes met mine. "Picture Caspar."

Opening and closing my fist, I punched the bag again and again. Anger came from places I didn't know existed. It wasn't just anger toward Caspar, but toward myself, toward my parents, even Galton. It was anger at impossible situations.

"Hey guys," Briar interrupted from the doorway. "Come with me."

Ever grabbed me. "You okay?"

I nodded.

We followed Briar to the med bay. A body was lying on the bed dressed in a silver uniform. Ever stepped closer and examined the AI. "Flawless," she commented.

"Do you approve?"

"She looks great. Does she work?"

Briar smiled. "We're about to find out." She rolled the AI over, pulled her shirt up just enough to slip a tiny microchip into the hidden drive under her arm. Seconds later, the AI's eyes popped open revealing their green color and she sat up. Her gaze shifted over each of us.

"Hello, Nirvana crew." She looked down at her hands, flipped them over and back again. "You have given me a body."

"Yes, Zia," Briar answered. "I hope you're happy with what I picked."

"This is very nice. Thank you." She stood and walked to a mirror where she placed her long auburn hair in a bun. She turned to Ever and said, "I am ready for duty."

"I'm going to let Briar show you around or whatever it is she has planned," Ever responded.

"Wow!" I said when we were alone again. "I knew AIs were advanced, but she's amazing. So humanlike." My mind started wandering to my nanites. How much like her was I? Did the nanites only heal me? Did they do more? Could they?

"You're lost in your thoughts again."

My eyes met hers and I shrugged. "Sorry."

She opened her mouth like she was going to say more, but instead she leaned in and kissed me.

Ever excused herself to do a few ship related things, so I wandered around. I found Zabe in the observation room stroking Nero who was purring in his lap. Zabe looked more approachable holding a cute animal.

Nero's eyes opened as I plopped down next to them. "Traitor," I said, sticking out my tongue. Nero just closed his eyes again. I laughed.

"You're good for us," Zabe said.

"I am?"

"Yes. You're the calm in the storm."

Staring into the dark space, I said, "You're all good people, Zabe, just in a bad situation."

"I tried telling Caspar no once. That was when he killed my brother. Two guards had to hold me back. He was just a kid."

I couldn't imagine going through that. Bristow was like my brother and I didn't know what I would do if something ever happened to him. "I'm sorry, Zabe. Caspar's gone now. He can't hurt anybody else."

"You're brave, Akacia. Stupid, but brave." He smiled. "Everleigh has been through a lot. Be patient with her."

I stood up, tousled Zabe's hair. He looked up, shocked that I had dared to be so familiar with him. His expression melted into a smile and I left to wander some more.

***

Huxley cooked meat and vegetables for dinner. We all ate quietly.

"This is delicious," I told him.

"Thanks, Akacia." His smile was sad. "These guys are so used to my cooking, they don't appreciate it anymore. It was nice to cook for someone else."

"I've enjoyed all of your meals." I blinked back the tears.

"I suppose I should tell you what I am, too?" Zabe said out of the blue.

Reaching across the table, I placed my hand on his. "Only if you want to tell me."

He took a swig of his drink. "Black bear. I'm strong and quick-tempered."

"Don't bother him when he's sleeping. He may bite your head off," Ever joked.

Zabe growled at her and she laughed.

My emotions began to overwhelm me so I dabbed my mouth with my napkin and said, "Thank you all for opening up to me and making me feel like part of your family. You will always be a part of mine." And before I broke down completely, I stood up and walked back toward the sleeping quarters.

I stopped in front of Ever's room, unsure if I should go find her or wait for her in my own room. Of course, I hadn't been in my room since the first night back.

"I gave you access to my room," Ever said from behind me. "Just put your hand on the pad."

I did as she said and the door opened. Inside, I sat on the bed and rubbed her blanket in between my thumb and forefinger.

Ever knelt in front of me. "It'll be okay."

"It's not just that."

"Then what is it?"

Blowing out a long deep breath, I said, "I'll miss you…all of you." Then I added, "I'll be home tomorrow and I'll have to be the Empress again. Tonight, I'm just Kaci. That's it. Nothing special. I want to be with you." I could feel the burn in my cheeks. "Not necessarily sex. I just want to be next to you. Can we do that?"

"Yes, except for one thing."

"What?" I looked up.

"You *are* special."

Tears brimmed my eyes.

I changed into the cami and took everything else off besides my underwear, then climbed in bed. Tears soaked my pillow.

When Ever climbed into bed behind me I closed my eyes. Her warmth, her touch, it was what I needed right now. A wave of shivers rolled down my spine at the feel of her warm breath on the back of my neck. I was soothed by her closeness.

Ever put her arm over my side and a soft hum escaped from me. The safe feeling surrounded me. I wanted her to feel that way, too. To know she could tell me anything.

"I saw the cages."

Ever's body stiffened.

"You don't have to say anything. I just wanted you to know that you can."

Her response was soft, almost non-existent. "Thank you."

She didn't say anything else and that was okay. I just had to make sure she knew that I could be her safe place, just like she was mine.

CHAPTER TWENTY-FOUR

AKACIA

WHEN WE WOKE, THE MOOD was somber. Ever shuffled to the bathroom and got ready. She left her hair down and put on very little makeup. I took my time getting prepared. As glad as I was to be going home, I was heartbroken to leave. Ever didn't say anything during breakfast or on the way to the bridge. It was as if talking would hurt.

"Briar? What's the news on Caspar's ship?" Ever inquired.

"Reports are saying an internal explosion destroyed the ship. No talk of foul play," she responded. "I'll keep listening. I do have some news on the tracking device."

Ever's head snapped up. "What?"

"It looks like it's been on there a while. I think Caspar put it on the ship when he handed it over to us. He's always been keeping track of us, we just didn't know. We never had a reason to disobey him before."

"You never realized it was there when you hacked the ship to take control?"

Briar shook her head. "No. I'm sorry."

"It's okay. Are you sure it was the only one?"

"Yes. I did a sweep of the ship and I asked Lael to verify it was the only one."

Ever seemed to be lost in thought as she doodled on paper.

"Can you hail Valinor?" I asked.

Briar pushed a few buttons and then Galton appeared on the screen.

"Empress."

"Galton. We will be arriving shortly."

"Who exactly?"

"Whoever I decide to bring with me, Galton. I expect you to treat them as guests."

He gave a firm nod and the screen went black.

"I think it would be best if just you came at first," I said to Ever.

"We can jump down."

"Okay."

Out the window, I could see Valinor getting closer and closer. The planet was beautiful from afar. White clouds swirled above the blues, greens, and purples. That was my home, my planet. My people were waiting for me.

"Are you sure about this?" Ever asked, holding the jump device.

"Yes."

Ever put in her earpiece and led me to the jump circle. Nero joined us. Seconds later, we were standing in the grass just outside the compound. Closing my eyes, I took a deep breath and filled my lungs with the familiar scents around me. Home.

Ever was checking in with the rest of the crew. "We're fine. Stay there."

I heard the door open and opened my eyes to see Galton standing before me. His eyes shifted to Ever and a scowl came over his face.

"Galton," I said to get his attention.

He smiled, approached, and took my hands. "Empress. I'm so glad you're home."

"Thank you."

"Kaci!" Bristow came running around the corner, picked me up, and spun me around. "You're really okay?"

"I am."

He gave me a big bear hug. "Good. I'm tired of running this place. It's hard and quite boring."

Laughing, I messed his hair. "I'd say you did good a job. The planet is still here."

"And now I'm placing her back in your hands." He gave a slight nod and I kicked him. "I tried my best to find you. I just didn't do it in time."

"It all worked out."

He nodded. "So who did you bring down here?"

My eyes flicked to Ever. "Galton, Bristow, this is Everleigh. She is here as my guest."

Galton huffed. "She's the one who turned you over to Caspar. The reason you crashed on that planet. And the reason you were almost sold back to him."

"Galton, I appreciate your concern, but it is none of your business."

Bristow at least was understanding. "Hi, Everleigh. I'm Bristow. Kaci's best friend." He stuck out his hand and Ever shook it.

"Kaci has told me about you."

He grinned. "She has?"

"Something like best friends and partners in crime."

Galton cleared his throat and Ever looked like she was caught doing something wrong, but Bristow laughed.

"That we are. I'm glad she didn't forget about me while amongst the stars. Speaking of which, weren't you the one who didn't want me to leave and then you decided to go off adventuring?"

"Wasn't exactly voluntarily, but I won't hold you back, Bristow. I told you that before. I will miss you, but I want you to be happy."

A smile spread across his face. "You are the best."

"I know."

Nero, who had been on Ever's back, climbed onto my shoulder.

"What is that?" Bristow asked.

"This is Nero. He hitchhiked back with us from Terronda."

"Does he bite?"

"I'm sure he does, but he hasn't bitten us."

Bristow shot me a look, but then smiled, and held out his hand. Nero looked at me and I nodded and said, "He's okay."

Nero then jumped onto Bristow's arm and crawled up to his neck sniffing him. Bristow laughed and tried to get him back in his hands.

"I hate to interrupt, but there are things that need to be attended to," Galton stated.

"Bristow, could you entertain Everleigh while I catch up with Galton?"

"Of course," Bristow responded with a smile.

"Don't go too far. I want you both to join me in a few minutes."

In the command center, everyone welcomed me back. Vika gave me a hug. "I'm so glad you're okay. We were all very worried about you."

"Thank you, Vika." Speaking loud enough for everyone in

the room to hear, I continued, "You all did a wonderful job taking care of Valinor. As your Empress, I thank you."

Galton went over everything that had taken place since I had been gone. The weather had been mostly good, but one storm caused some damage.

"One of the dams broke, but we got it fixed and water supply has been good since. Food is growing. President Loera of Flion wants to set up trading. And Hettie passed away," Galton reported.

"Oh, no. She was a lovely lady."

"Her daughter has taken over the shop."

"I'll stop and see her. I also want to see the families of those who died when the Razor was destroyed."

Galton brought me up to speed on a bunch of small things that had happened in my absence. I was beginning to think he was stalling. "We need to talk, Galton. Can we go into the conference room?"

"Shall I get Vika?" Galton asked.

"No. I'd prefer it just to be the four of us." I waved to Bristow and Ever as we entered the room. "Please, join us at the table."

"You want me to be here?" Ever asked.

"Yes."

She followed and sat next to me.

"I need some answers, Galton, and I'm hoping you have them for me. I should be dead, but for some reason, I healed. What do you know about that?"

Galton swallowed, but Bristow was the one who spoke first. "What do you mean?"

"I mean exactly what I said. First Caspar tortured me and

then we crashed on a planet. I was also shot by a guard in Terronda. Yet, I don't have a mark on me. I healed."

The three of us looked at Galton waiting for him to say something. He seemed reluctant to speak and it angered me.

"Let me tell you what I know. I have nanites. What I don't know is why."

Galton took a deep breath. "Your father, Atlas, was a brilliant scientist as you know. He had perfected using nanites to heal someone and word got out. We're not sure how or by who. While your father was working, you were running around playing when someone broke in trying to get the nanites. Bristow's father, Braylon ran in with a couple of guards. There was a firefight with the intruder. Nobody realized you were in the room and you got hit in the crossfire. The intruder was killed and you were critically injured. Your mother pleaded with your father to help. The nanites hadn't been tested on a child, but he agreed and put them in you."

"And I healed."

"You healed."

"Why didn't he or someone tell me?" I asked, my voice shaky. When Ever put her hand on mine, it didn't go unnoticed.

Galton forced his eyes back on my face before continuing. "I'm sure he was going to—"

"But he died, Galton! He died and you helped raise me and never mentioned it. I have *machines* running through my body."

"I'm sorry, Empress. I only had your best interest at heart. You never really got hurt after that, but anytime you fell down and healed quickly, I waited for the questions. They never came."

"I never asked. You never told."

"I figured I would when you stepped into your own, but something was always going on. There's no excuse. I apologize." He looked away, tears brimming in his eyes.

"What if something had happened? A side effect of some sort."

"I figured it was fine. It had been years since your father injected you and there had been none."

Bristow reached over and took the hand that Ever wasn't holding. "I know you, Kace. I know what you're thinking. This doesn't change who you are." His eyes were sympathetic and he gave me a half-smile.

"That's what I told her," Ever said.

"They're right, Empress. You're no less of a person." Galton tried to sound reassuring.

"No. I'm something more." I sighed. "I want the details of what went down when my parents were killed."

Bristow sat up in his seat. This concerned him, too. We had talked about it plenty of times, but neither of us asked for the particulars before.

"The details?"

"Yes."

"You know them. Late one night, your parents were in the lab when it was attacked."

"You told me that my parents were killed because someone was trying to take over the planet, but that's not exactly true, is it?"

Galton stroked his chin for a minute before taking a deep breath. "People had tried to get their hands on Valinor—that part was true. You've seen that happen yourself. But, no, your parents' deaths were not for that reason. Atlas, Braylon, and Raysel had been in the lab all day working on Project Infinity. With the nanites and another success—"

"Splicers?" I guessed.

Galton's eyes widened and he nodded. "Yes, with the success of the nanites and the Splicers, he was researching something new. Your mother had gone in to check on him, convince him to get some rest. A team of four highly trained assassins attacked. Your father always had a plan. With the push of a button, the computers were wiped clean and a self-destruct began. They tried to fight their way out, but the lab exploded before they could. Your parents, Bristow's parents, and the four assassins were killed in the blast."

"Why did he have to blow it up?"

"So everything would be destroyed, so nobody could get their hands on his research. Your father was a good man, Empress. He did not want his experiments and discoveries to be used for bad things. He wanted to keep you safe. He knew whoever hired those men would want to know who he tested the experiments on and that would lead them to you. He feared that you would be abducted."

"Like the Splicer children. Caspar was the one who captured them, turned them into thieves, and used them to do his dirty work. He wanted me because he thought I had knowledge of these experiments."

"What did you tell him?"

"Nothing. I don't know anything. Did anything survive the blast?"

"The lab was destroyed."

"What about anyone else who worked with them?" I probed.

"I'm not a scientist. Sometimes your father would ramble about something, but I could never make heads or tails of what he was saying. Atlas kept most of the big things to himself. He and Braylon. You could talk to Ode and Curt. They were his assistants." Galton met my eyes. "I'm sorry that I don't have more answers for you. I know how frustrating it is. Your father was a friend to me. I miss him everyday."

"Tell me what you know of the Splicers," I asked.

"There were twenty sets of parents who volunteered to bear children. They were sent to live about a hundred miles away along with any family, just in case the children were more animalistic than they were supposed to be. They were to raise their children and train them how to use their animal senses to protect others. When they were adults, they would have made great warriors or guards. They too were attacked and nobody was left."

"What happened to them?"

"Some were killed, the others abducted."

"Where did they find the volunteers?"

"All of the volunteers came from right here, Empress."

I stole a look at Ever, who looked just as shocked to hear this news. She and her whole crew were originally from Valinor.

"What was Project Infinity?" I asked curiously.

Galton hesitated, clearly not comfortable with this topic. "Your father was working on finding a way to extend life."

"Immortality?"

"More like slowing the aging process down, scanning DNA and correcting undesirable genetic conditions, enhancing DNA, and downloading one mind into another carrier."

"Whoa…" Ever said.

Whoa was right! I had no idea what to think of this. I understood when Galton said my father was a good man and tried to create things that would be helpful, but all of the things he created could be dangerous in the wrong hands. I was beginning to think it was a good thing everything was destroyed.

"Galton?" Ever asked.

"Yes?"

"Did you ever figure out who the leak was?"

I hadn't thought of that.

"No." His answer was simple, but terrifying.

"So most likely there's a traitor among us," I said softly, like all of a sudden we weren't safe.

"I guess that's one way to look at it. We haven't had any trouble since that day."

"Of course not. There was never anything to leak."

"Unless the leak is the one who told Caspar that Kaci might have information," Bristow said. "Think about it. If the leak believes Kaci knows something, he or she could have told Caspar and that's why she was abducted."

"But I don't know anything."

"This person must think you do."

"Or it could have been a coincidence," Galton said.

"Caspar's dead. That doesn't matter. However, having someone who is not loyal does concern me. Galton, can you quietly arrange for a couple of people you trust to look into this?"

"As you wish, Empress."

Galton returned to the command center and Bristow had something to do, or so he said. My mind was reeling from these new developments. Part of me wished I hadn't come back, but when I looked at the horizon and just the joy of being outdoors in the fresh air, I knew this was where I belonged

"You okay?" Ever asked.

"I'm not sure." It was the most honest answer I had. We

walked around the compound. "Do you think the others would like to come down and see the planet?"

"Maybe. I can ask," Ever answered as she peeked in the rooms we passed. "So, where's your throne?"

I rolled my eyes. "I don't have a throne."

"Too bad."

My eyes shot over to her at the deep tone in her voice. "Would seeing me sitting on a throne be a turn on for you?"

She took a step closer. "I guess we'll never know."

Just before our lips touched, Bristow walked in. "Oh, sorry."

Ever just smiled and said, "I'm going to check in with Briar. See if they want to come."

Bristow cornered me while Ever talked to Briar. "So…you two?"

My cheeks warmed. "Yeah."

"Just one question, Kace."

"What?"

"She worked for the enemy. I've seen her criminal log. Why her? What's so awesome about her?"

What could I say? How could I possibly explain everything she was to me? Everything she wasn't? There were no words to make someone else understand. "Do you trust me, Bristow?"

"Of course."

"Then trust me on this. Things aren't always as they seem. Not everything is black and white. There is both good and evil in everyone." I thought about killing Caspar and his man. "It's a long story and I'll tell you about it later, but right now, just trust me."

He squeezed my hand. "As long as you're happy."

"Thanks."

"Good luck with Galton."

Ever and I waited with Galton and Bristow for Briar and Huxley to jump down.

Briar's face was lit up the moment their feet hit the ground. "It smells so lovely."

Huxley rolled his eyes. "I like the compound idea. Doesn't look like much, but I bet it is inside."

"Galton, Bristow, this is Huxley and Briar," I introduced.

"Guys, this is Galton, my second-in-command right now, and Bristow, my best friend and family."

Galton stood there scowling, but Bristow extended his hand and I didn't miss the way he held Briar's longer, or the blush on his cheeks, or the way she smiled.

"Don't they have any manners?" Galton growled. "Bow before the Empress!"

I didn't have time to say anything before Huxley replied, "What?"

"It is customary to bow before the leaders of a planet when you are on their planet. It shows you respect them and will obey their laws." Galton's eyes looked like they were going to bulge out of his head.

I put up my hand to stop him from saying anything further. "Enough!"

"Empress, this is not appropriate!"

"I said enough." My hands clenched and unclenched. "Galton, may I talk to you for a minute. And don't mistake that for anything less than an order."

We stepped out of earshot.

"I understand your anger toward them. I even get that you don't trust them yet. But I do and I need you to trust me. If you can't, you need to excuse yourself so that you're not around my guests. You will treat them with respect. They do not need to bow. You know I have never been one for such formalities."

When I finished, Galton took a moment before responding, "I understand, Empress, and will obey your wishes to stay away. But I will be keeping an eye on them because I vowed to look after you."

"I do appreciate it, Galton."

Back with the crew of the Nirvana, I apologized, "I'm sorry for Galton's behavior. He's very protective and traditional. Where is Zabe?"

"Someone had to stay with the ship," Huxley answered.

Bristow and I showed my new friends around Valinor until the sunstar went down. We visited the lake where Bristow and I skipped stones, the farmlands, the village, the schools, and around the compound.

"There's plenty of room here if you wanted to stay," I heard myself saying. It wasn't something I had planned. It just kind of came out.

Briar was the first one to answer. "We have to find our families first. Only then can we think about where home is."

"I know. I just wanted to offer. I wanted you all to know you're welcome here."

"It's a great place, Akacia. Thank you for such an offer," Huxley said with a warm smile.

Ever had a different kind of look on her face. She was upset. "What?"

"You're forgetting an important detail," she said.

"Being?"

"We're wanted criminals. You would be charged with harboring fugitives."

"Oh. There is that," Huxley commented.

"Maybe the Authority would listen to reason. Since Caspar is dead, you won't be doing these things anymore, right?" My gaze shifted to each of them.

"Right," Briar answered and I wondered why Ever hadn't spoken up. "But I don't think the Authority is going to pardon every crime we've ever committed."

She was probably dead-on, but I hated it. It wasn't right. Caspar was finally out of the way and they still couldn't live their lives. They'd always be on the run.

A big feast had been prepared for my return and Ever, Briar, and Huxley stayed as my guests. Bristow sat across from Briar. I noticed them stealing glances at each other throughout the meal.

"Not bad," Huxley said with a smirk.

"You could stay and teach them a thing or two," I teased, but part of me wished he'd take me up on it.

"It'll give you a reason to come visit us."

"She's definitely just going to visit for your eggs, Hux," Briar joked.

Ever was unusually quiet.

"The eggs are absolutely a reason to visit," I joked. Turning to Ever, I said, "Will you stay just tonight?"

"Kaci, I—"

"I know you have to get going, but it's just the night. You can leave at first light. I just…please. I want one more night."

She reached out and touched my face. "Alright." Facing Briar and Huxley, she told them to return to the ship and she'd be back in the morning.

Briar hugged me first. "I'm sorry about the whole handing you over thing. I am glad to call you a friend."

"Me, too." I squeezed her tight. "Tell Zabe I said goodbye."

"I will."

Huxley was next. "There will always be eggs for you."

Hugging him, I said, "There better be." In his ear, I whispered, "Take care of her."

He pulled back and looked me right in the eyes. "I always do."

"Fare thee well," I said, giving them Valinor's goodbye saying.

"Safe journey," Briar and Huxley said back, then disappeared.

Just as we turned to walk away, I heard, "Akacia!"

"Zabe?" I spun back around.

"Did you really think you'd get off without saying goodbye to me?"

"So you do care?" I teased.

Never one for many words, he wrapped his big arms around me and squeezed. And that told me everything I needed to know. He cared.

After Zabe was gone, I took Ever by the hand and led her to my bedroom. Nero trailed behind. She looked around the room, studying everything from the books to the pictures of my parents to what was in my closet.

I reached out and jerked her toward me, crushing my lips against hers. She whimpered against my mouth. I walked her backward until we fell onto my bed.

The kisses were long and slow as if we had all the time in the world to do nothing but kiss. My hands cradled her face wanting to keep her as close to me as possible. We were panting when we broke the kiss, but instead of parting, we stared into each other's eyes.

I traced the curve of her neck with my lips. A pleasant sigh escaped between her parted lips. Pushing me onto my back, she dropped kisses on my abdomen and then swirled her tongue around my navel.

Warmth started to spread in my stomach and a tingling settled between my legs. I wanted her. I wanted to explore every inch of her body and have her know every part of mine. I wanted to know what would make her smile and which things would elicit a moan. My hands wandered to her hips, thumbs resting just above the waistband of her pants. She sucked in a shuddering breath.

"Kaci…" she whispered. "I want nothing more than to make love to you, but I'm leaving tomorrow. I won't do that to you."

"What if I want you to?"

"I'll still say no. You deserve better, Kaci. You're special."

"Then don't leave." I knew she needed to go, but I had to say it.

She closed her eyes and brought her lips back to mine for a hungrier, more desperate kiss. "I have to."

"I know." I lifted my head so my lips could meet hers again. If she wouldn't make love to me, I was going to take all the kisses I could. I wanted to remember how her lips felt on mine, how she tasted, how I could see the love in her eyes. "Take your pants off."

"Kaci—"

"I just want you to lay with me and I want to feel your skin on mine. This is our last night together, I want to remember, Ever. Please." A tear slipped out of the corner of my eye.

She kissed it away. "Okay."

We lay facing each other in my bed, staring into each other's eyes. Not needing words. Just being there. Together. Eventually, I rolled over and let her hold me.

CHAPTER TWENTY-FIVE

EVERLEIGH

AT FIRST LIGHT, MY EYES popped open. I breathed in Kaci's scent while she was still in my arms. I didn't want to wake her, but I had to go. It would be easier if I just slipped away, but I didn't want to. I wanted to stay with her, be with her, love her forever. But I knew I had obligations to my crew, my people, and I couldn't put her in danger. Not only from the Authority, but from me. I had changed her. She wasn't a sweet, innocent girl anymore. I'd never forgive myself for that.

"I love you," I whispered, carefully getting up and taking one last look at her. Then I snuck out the door.

I found Bristow and Galton in the command center. Galton glared, while Bristow smiled. "You don't have to worry about me. I'm leaving now. I know I don't need to tell you this, but take care of her."

Galton's face relaxed. "Of course."

"May I talk to you?" I asked Bristow.

He nodded and followed me over to a corner of the room. "What's up?"

"I didn't want to tell Galton this. He wouldn't accept it.

If she ever needs help or if Valinor ever needs anything, please contact me."

Bristow nodded. "You care for her."

"I do. Very much." I turned to go, but then looked back. "She's been having panic attacks. You have to get her to focus and breathe when she has them."

"Panic attacks?"

"Since Caspar tortured her."

He nodded understanding. "Thank you for telling me."

"You're welcome."

Outside, I pulled out the jump device.

"Wait!" I stopped hearing the lovely voice, but didn't turn around.

She came up behind me and wrapped me in her arms. Nestling her face in my neck, she kissed me. I let out a breath I didn't know I had been holding. As if she could tell how I was feeling, she turned me around and we stared into each other's eyes. All I saw was love. Even though I had hurt her, betrayed her, tried to make her hate me, and was now walking away from her, she still loved me.

I opened my mouth to ask why, but she put her finger to my lips.

"Shhh."

Our eyes locked. Her lips met mine like she was a force to be reckoned with. My own lips didn't hold back and seconds later my arms held her close to me. The kiss wasn't brief or gentle. It was messy and desperate. It was begging for more. It was longing and angst. Salt from our tears mixed in with her sweet honey taste. I was slightly dazed when we pulled apart.

Holding her gaze, I cupped her cheek tenderly. I wanted to jump back to the Nirvana with her. Wanted to stay here. Wanted to be with her. She was it for me. She was my everything. My soul mate. The one true love of my life. I would never find someone like her again. I didn't even want to try. If I couldn't have her, I didn't want anyone. I was hers. Forever.

But forever would never be.

Kaci wiped away a tear that fell down my cheek. "I told you this when you were unconscious, but I figured I should tell you when you can actually hear me. I wanted to hate you, but instead I fell in love with you."

"Kaci—"

"You don't have to say anything. We don't know what tomorrow will bring, so I just wanted you to know." She was blinking a lot, fighting back her own tears. "Will you come back?"

"I don't know."

"You could."

"Being here would put you—all of you—in danger."

"We'll figure it out."

"I can't."

"You'd give all this up?" She pointed to the planet, knowing I would enjoy exploring the different parts of it.

"You could come with me," I said, unable to control myself. She'd still be in danger on my ship, but she'd be one of us.

"I can't."

"You'd give up all that?" I pointed to the stars.

"I belong here."

"And I belong there. I have to look for my people. I have to find them."

"I know." She wiped away a tear that managed to escape. "So that's it? Our feelings don't matter?"

"We're so different. It probably wouldn't work anyway." I swallowed hard.

"Right. Then go without hesitation. Live your life to the fullest. Tomorrow is not promised. Safe journey." She stepped back and her bottom lip trembled.

I hated walking away from her. Hated it. But it was the right thing to do. I let her go with a whole lot of hesitation. "Fare thee well," I said, reciting the Valinor goodbye.

I claimed her lips one last time and then pushed the jump drive and was back on my ship. I didn't see her sobbing as she crumpled to the ground and she didn't see me do the same.

The End
Painted Skies: Beyond Earth Book Two Available

READ ON FOR A PREVIEW OF

THE
ULTIMATE
SACRIFICE
BOOK ONE OF THE GIFTED TEENS SERIES

TALIA JAGER

CHAPTER ONE

KASSIA

J ANA STOOD IN FRONT OF me, her hands waving frantically in my face. My gift had taken over, and I could no longer hear her screaming. Jana had never liked me and she tried everything to piss me off. She wasn't even a student at our school, but she had dated a few of the boys here. Although she was one of the increasing number of normal humans aware of us, she had no idea what my gift was, and that I could easily drop her to her knees in pain.

I narrowed my eyes and focused on her. She suddenly stopped yelling at me and began to rub her temples. I could feel my temperature rise as the anger continued to build in me. A small smile flickered across my face as I felt her pain building.

"Stop!" Mira yelled and jumped in between Jana and me. "She's not worth it! Don't let her push your buttons!"

I mashed my lips. Pity that my best friend was immune to my gift. Nobody knew why this was. It wasn't her only talent; she was also a compeller. She could tell someone what to do and that person would do it. There had been many times I wished I could have had her gift instead of mine. All I had to do was wish someone to be in pain and within a minute, they were.

When I saw the concern in Mira's eyes, I let up. She let out a sigh of relief and turned to Jana. "Go home, Jana. You were never here."

Jana turned and slowly began to pace away in a daze with a confused look on her face.

"Sorry," I muttered, ashamed that I let my gift get the best of me again.

"You know how annoying this is getting? You need better self-control."

"You sound like my counselor."

"Maybe I should be."

I felt like smacking her, but she'd just smack me back, and she hit harder than I did.

We got in the car and took the two-lane road back to campus, which was nestled in the mountains in northern California. I glanced out the window at the towering trees on both sides of us. The moon had just peeked over the tops of the trees, lighting the way home.

After twenty minutes, the trees thinned out and before us stood Glendale Institute, one of two "gifted" schools in the country. Glendale was made up of a cluster of buildings enclosed by lush forests.

We parked in the parking lot and hiked up toward the courtyard. Directly across from the parking lot was a training field. As we entered the courtyard, there were dorms on our left and right, one for girls, one for boys. Straight ahead were the faculty quarters, dining hall, and learning center.

Each L-shaped dorm had two wings. The longer side housed the high school–aged students, and the shorter side was for the middle school students. When we walked into the room we shared, Mira told me, "Go to bed."

"You don't need to mother me."

"Well, someone does and since nobody else is stepping up to the plate, I kind of have to."

"What's your deal?"

Her eyes narrowed. "I happened to be with someone when you went all mental."

Oh. That's what this was about. "You met a guy?"

"Yeah, a cute one, and you had to go and ruin it." She sighed. "I rushed out of there so fast when Noe called I didn't get his number."

Guilt washed over me. "I'm sorry, Mira."

Her face relaxed a little. "I know."

"I didn't mean to get so mad. She just…infuriates me." I got angry just thinking about the little tramp.

"You have to learn how to ignore some things."

I stuck out my tongue. "Pbbbbbt."

"Do you know what could happen if you actually hurt someone?" she asked, raising her voice.

I pulled my hair back into a ponytail. "I'd feel good?"

"No, Kassia. You'd get in trouble. They'd punish you. And then they'd punish me for not stopping you."

"Okay, okay, I'll try to do better."

"You said that last time."

"Oh yeah. But that guy deserved it!"

She guffawed. "Yeah, he did." She broke into a grin and we both collapsed on the floor laughing.

I watched Mira as she slept, wishing I could sleep like she did. The nightmares usually woke me up. At first, it was only once in a while, but now it was every night. Mira's long, ash-blonde hair was spread all over her pillow. Her thin lips twitched now and then. She was my protector, although I think she spent most of her time protecting other people from me.

Sometimes I felt like I was broken. I had this rare gift, but instead of using it to do good, I used it for the wrong reasons. There have only been ten of us documented in history. Ten mind-blowers. Some were locked up because nobody could control them. Others were killed for the same reason. A few were able to control their gifts. And then there was me. I had Mira.

All of the students here at Glendale Institute had gifts. Some gifts—like mine—were only supposed to be used in emergencies. However, with my short temper, I don't think the gods planned that one out real well.

How then did Mira get to me so fast? Noe. She was a predictor and could see things that hadn't happened yet. Mira said Noe had called and tipped her off. Although we had driven to the town center together, we went our separate ways when we got there. We needed to be quick so we'd be back to Glendale before curfew.

As dawn approached and the sky brightened with yellows and oranges, I snuck back into bed, quietly pulled the covers up over my head, and pretended to be asleep. One minute later, the alarm clock went off. I heard Mira groan and hit the nightstand as her hand searched for the off button. Finally, the alarm stopped.

"Kassia, time to get up." She shook my arm.

I moaned. "Okay."

"We can get to the bathroom before anyone else if you hurry."

Slowly, I emerged from under the covers, rubbed my eyes,

and yawned. It was some of my best acting yet. "What are we waiting for? Let's go."

Mira shot me a look and then smiled. We headed down to the bathroom we shared with the two other girls in the hall. I went straight to one of the showers and turned the water up hot.

A few minutes later, Mira called out for me. "Did you fall asleep in there?"

"No, I fell in the drain."

"Funny," she said, her voice droll.

I sighed and turned the shower off. I towel-dried my hair and body and slipped on my T-shirt and shorts again. Then I brushed my teeth. The rest I could do in our room.

As we were leaving, Noe and Auralee walked in. "Hey, Kassia, did you leave some hot water for the rest of us?" Auralee asked. She always looked beautiful no matter what time of day it was. Her strawberry blonde, pixie-like haircut required no styling at all.

I laughed. "Of course, but Mira didn't." Mira scowled at me. "Oh, lighten up." I elbowed her.

"Not before noon," she mumbled.

Back in our room, I unwrapped my hair and stood in front of the mirror for a long time. Same old dark auburn hair, glaring white skin. At least I didn't have pimples. They wouldn't dare show themselves.

"Were you expecting something different?" Mira asked, standing next to me. I was about half an inch taller, and a few pounds heavier.

"No." I couldn't tell her about my nightmares, about how sometimes I'd change into something awful in them. She'd worry too much. Besides, they were just nightmares.

I fumbled around the dresser for my eye shadow and lipstick—a light purple that brought out my eyes. Mira chose green eye shadow and a light pink lipstick.

"Purple again?" She rolled her eyes. They would most likely be categorized as hazel, but when you looked closer, you would see they were a blue-green, with specs of gold and brown floating in them.

"Violet," I corrected.

"Whatever."

"It matches."

I smiled smugly. My eyes were truly a light violet color. Being curious, I once did some research and found that violet eyes were rare to both the gifted and regular humans.

I pulled on my gray school sweatshirt, which was a little bit long in the arms, just the way I liked it. I always bought my long-sleeved shirts long enough to cover at least half of my hands.

"Ready for breakfast?" Mira asked.

"Yeah. Are you looking forward to seeing Zane?"

She blushed and bit her lip. "He's not my type." Her nose wrinkled—a sign she was lying.

ABOUT THE AUTHOR

 When Talia isn't hiding in the bathroom from her six children munching on a chocolate bar, she enjoys hiking the red rocks in Utah or sitting on the beach with a Kindle in her hands and her toes in the ocean. She firmly believes that love is love and hopes the acceptance shown in this book will become canon someday.

Talia has written a number of books including *Damaged: Natalie's Story, Teagan's Story: Her Battle With Epilepsy, If I Die Young, Secret Bloodline, Lost and Found, Falling for Fire, Touch of Death* and *The Gifted Teens Series*. She also co-wrote *The Between Worlds Series* and *Mesmerized*.

Connect with Talia online at http://www.taliajager.com
Talia's blog: http://taliajager.blogspot.com
Facebook: http://www.facebook.com/taliajager
Twitter: http://www.twitter.com/taliajager
Instagram: @TaliaJager

Made in the USA
Middletown, DE
30 January 2020